How to Update Your Parents

Pete Johnson

Also available:

ISBN 978-1-78270-160-6

For Phoebe – a big fan of Louis the Laugh

ISBN 978-1-78270-172-9

First published by Award Publications Limited 2016

Published by Award Publications Limited, The Old Riding School, The Welbeck Estate, Worksop, Nottinghamshire, S80 3LR

17 3

Printed in the United Kingdom

Legendary comic Louis the Laugh

Geography book

bin

Chapter One

No More School

Tuesday December 24th (Christmas Eve)

3.25 p.m.

I've just chucked all my geography books away.

But don't you dare feel sorry for them, as they've totally brought it on themselves.

Every day of this Christmas holiday, they've been lolling in my bedroom, smirking away about the bucket loads of homework I've got to do.

Until today – when I couldn't take any more. So I've hurled them into the rubbish bin next to a gang of teabags and something very brown and highly stinky, which I hope is soup. And already my room feels bigger, happier.

3

Only when I go back to school I'm going to be in so much trouble, aren't I? So why on earth did I do it?

Am I mad?

Probably. But there's something you should know about me.

I'm Louis – also known as Louis the Laugh – because even when I was four I was telling silly jokes like:

What does a unicorn call its father?
Popcorn.

Well, it made my aunties chuckle. And it sparked a dream deep inside me. Perhaps one day I could be a comedian. But I didn't move one millimetre nearer to my dream until ... I met Maddy.

She's my girlfriend. Been on three whole dates now. Impressive, I know.

But Maddy's also my agent. She's only my age (thirteen) but she knows tons and tons about show business. And she was the one who helped get me on to the top TV talent show, *Kids with Attitude*.

I made it all the way to the final as well. And if I won that I'd have my own half hour show. No wonder I practised and practised until the big day when ... my mobile's ringing.

I'd better take this. But I'll be back.

3.45 p.m.

Sorry about that, but it was Maddy. I'll tell you what she said in a second. But anyway, where was I?

Oh yeah – the day of the final. Well, I woke up with the vilest, vomitiest bug ever. And I really should have spent the day with my head in a bucket. But I couldn't miss the biggest chance of my whole life, could I? So I slogged to the studio, where the show was being broadcast live and then ...

Here's a little tip for you – if you ever get to the final of a TV talent show, don't stagger on to the stage and immediately throw up over the host. It distracts attention from your act for a start.

In fact, I never got the chance to tell even one joke, that shaming moment went viral and I acquired a wonderful new nickname at school – Vomit Boy. That was a bad time. And I hate bringing it up (sort of a joke there, sorry). Still, I didn't overreact. I just ran away from home, that's all. Only Maddy stopped me at the station. She had a message for me from Poppy.

Poppy won *Kids with Attitude*. She's a

magician who didn't let being in a wheelchair stop her from performing four magic tricks at once. Her prize, of course, was her own half hour TV show. But she was allowed one guest.

She chose me.

We recorded it a few days ago. I only had three minutes but I could have stayed out on that stage for three hours. And I left with the audience's laughter ringing in my ears. Best sound in the entire world.

The show goes out tonight – yes, that's right, Christmas Eve no less – at 5 p.m.

And Maddy – who, as I said, knows masses about show business – just called to tell me that even though it's Christmas Eve, my act is so good she is convinced the offers will pour in right away. And she wanted to make sure I was ready for that.

So am I ready to be off touring the world, leaving laughter behind me wherever I go? What do you think?

I know I might have to drop into school now and again, just to keep my hand in. So I'll pop by when I've got a couple of spare hours between flights. And I'll make certain that's never when I've got Geography.

*　　*　　*

4.05 p.m.

A lion goes into a restaurant. He sits down and the waiter asks if he'd like to order a starter.

'Yeah, I'll have the salmon please,' says the lion.

'And what would you like for your main?' asks the waiter.

And the lion replies, 'Oh, just a comb.'

That's the first joke you'll hear me say on television. And in less than an hour now!

4.07 p.m.

What do you get when you cross a bee with a giant ape?

Sting Kong.

That's my second joke. (Always follow a long joke with a really fast one.) I'll save the rest until after the show.

4.35 p.m.

Maddy's on her way to my house (she only lives three roads away). She's going to watch the show with my mum, dad and midget brother, Elliot.

Got tons of relations tuning in too. Plus anyone I've ever breathed near at school. Plus everyone I know on Facebook ... I didn't tell them to be super braggy, though. But this is a moment of history, isn't it?

4.40 p.m.
Maddy's arrived. And Mum and Dad have insisted she and I occupy the prime spot on the sofa. So I'm sitting here with my phone on my knee. Can't wait for it to start flashing. Only twenty minutes to go and I've never felt more excited.

6.50 p.m.
Maddy's just gone home and I'm sure you're keen to hear how the show went.

So please read on so you can see exactly what happened ...

Chapter Two

Chapter Three
I Become Invisible

6.50 p.m.
That's right.

Nothing at all happened, because I was cut from the show.

Let me just repeat that so the full horror can settle on you.

I. Was. Cut. From. The. Show.

I had no idea of the imminent catastrophe about to engulf me either.

So, we all watched Poppy perform her first trick. Then she was supposed to introduce me.

'I'm on next,' I said, desperately trying to sound chilled about it.

Only I wasn't on next at all.

The show jumped straight from Poppy performing her first trick to Poppy chatting with the audience.

'So where were you?' demanded Elliot at once.

'Ha, ha,' I began, then completely ran out of inspiration. Luckily Maddy chipped in. 'They've obviously rearranged the running order. It's very common in the world of television.'

'They're probably saving you to give the show a big ending,' said Dad.

'End with the best,' added Mum brightly.

Well there was no harm in hoping, was there? And my act would have made a cracking ending.

But twenty minutes later the show was over. Even then I had the tiniest wisp of hope that I might be seen right after the credits rushed past.

Only I wasn't.

I screwed my eyes shut tightly. This had to be a nightmare. Then I opened my eyes again. No, I was stuck with it. The most disappointing moment of my entire life. I hadn't a clue what to say either. Neither, it seemed, did anyone else. So that shocked, appalled silence just stretched and stretched and ...

'Hey, I'm filling up here!' I burst out at last. 'Anyone got a tissue? What in the name of Father Christmas is happening? Ha, ha.'

I said, 'Ha, Ha,' three or four times.

Then I saw I had a text from Evie at *Kids with Attitude*. She told me that the show had overrun by seven whole minutes, so they'd reluctantly had to make some cuts. Well, one cut mainly.

Me.

She hoped I wasn't too disappointed and wished me 'a really lovely Christmas'.

I was reading aloud her text when a large cake moved slowly into the living room. It was followed by Elliot. 'We can still eat it can't we?' he whined.

Emblazoned on the cake was 'CONGRATU-LATIONS, LOUIS THE LAUGH.' Yeah, it had my full name on it.

'It was going to be a little surprise,' whispered Mum. 'But you had no business bringing it out now, Elliot.'

'Why not?' I shouted. 'Come on, everyone, tuck in. It is Christmas after all.'

I've never eaten so much cake in my entire life. Couldn't tell you what it tasted like though.

8.00 p.m.

Lots of messages on my Facebook page already. Some were quite friendly – like the one from Theo, my best mate at my old school. 'I'm sure you'll be on another time. Be sure and let me know when.'

More typical though was: 'I blinked once and missed you, or were you so bad they couldn't show it?'

8.22 p.m.
Poppy's just called, practically in tears. 'I had no idea they were going to cut you.'

'I was pretty surprised too.'

'Oh Louis, I feel really terrible.'

'I bet I feel even worse,' I said.

Chapter Four

My Skateboarding Talent

Wednesday December 25th (Christmas Day)

Maddy's been round with my Christmas present. An incredible box set featuring all the top comedians of today. I gave her a charm bracelet, with hearts and stars on it. She said it was definitely her best Christmas present (and her other gifts included a new bike).

Then she said how much she admired the way I'd dealt with yesterday's shock event. 'Only a very superior person could have gone on making jokes – and eating all that cake.'

16

She added, 'It must be very hard being an undiscovered comedy star.'

I admitted that it was.

'But it will happen,' insisted Maddy. 'You *will* be discovered. It's just going to take a bit longer than we expected.'

Thursday December 26th

Invasion of the loons, otherwise known as our relations.

Great Aunt Betty, who is what can only be described as ancient, got the party swinging by raving on about the history of mistletoe. We have to pretend she doesn't tell us this every single Boxing Day.

This was followed by several centuries of board games.

Breaking News – Great Aunt Betty won at Monopoly. Not So Breaking News – she wins every single year. It's one of the laws of Christmas.

No one mentioned me not appearing on Poppy's show (I'm sure my parents had asked them not to) except Nan. As she was leaving she hissed that she was never watching that satellite channel again as they had treated me so disgracefully. 'Not that I ever watched it anyway,' she added. Still, I appreciated the gesture.

Friday December 27th

11.30 a.m.
'Not too disappointed, are you?' asked Dad,
plonking himself next to me.

'Oh no,' I lied.

'Remember, Louis, you've been in a TV studio
and you were judged good enough for them to
record you. Think of all the people who don't
even get that far.'

But that's what made it all the more
frustrating. To *almost* be on television. Then at
the very last second find yourself dumped.

'And who knows, something good may still
come from it,' said Dad.

Now I'm ever alert for silver linings but even
I couldn't think of one mildly good thing that
could occur now.

'It's all right, you know,' went on Dad, 'to be
fed up sometimes, especially when life doesn't
go the way you want it. Remember how I got a
bit fed up at the end of last year?'

I remembered.

In October Dad lost his job and Mum was
offered a full-time one. So they did a sort of
swap. And it was a total disaster – well, as far as

18

Dad was concerned it was. He cooked meals no one could even bear to look at, never mind eat, messed up the laundry and just about everything else. He even started getting lonely. So when I got home from school, instead of relaxing with a computer game, I had to talk to him instead. For several minutes!

'But you're all right now?' I asked.

'Oh definitely,' said Dad. 'Well, I've got all my courses to look forward to.'

Dad has joined a band of stay-at-home dads and has signed up for all sorts of courses specially designed for them.

'So we're all great,' I said staring meaningfully at the computer game Dad had interrupted.

Dad took the hint and got up but then said, 'You were very funny on Poppy's show, you know.'

I looked up. 'Yeah I was, wasn't I?'

'So you're a winner already in my eyes,' said Dad.

2.10 p.m.

I was casually listening to my parents twittering on about the bins being emptied (tragically, they really do talk about things like that) when I remembered that all my geography books were currently residing in one of those bin bags, due to be emptied any second.

I bombed outside. But of course it was Christmas, and there was a whole row of black bin bags massing about. How on earth was I going to find out which black bag they were in? So I began madly rooting through them all like some demented fox.

Finally, I hauled them out, now generously decorated with brown stains. And they didn't just smell. They stank. They reeked. Guaranteed to clear any room in seconds. So I sprayed them all over with Dad's after-shave. I even threw in a bit of hair spray as well.

I thought I'd very cunningly disguised their aroma. But later in my bedroom Maddy wasn't impressed. 'They smell so peculiar and what's that brown stuff over them?'

'Ancient soup probably, or, if not, well, you really don't want to know.'

'But Louis what made you put them in the bin?' she asked.

'I didn't put them in the bin, I hurled them in because they were annoying me so much and I didn't think ...'

'No, you didn't.'

'If you'd let me finish, I didn't think I'd need them anymore. Not after I'd been discovered. And what do you do with stuff you don't need any more? You dump it.'

'That's true,' agreed Maddy softly. 'I could always cover them,' she added.

'Hey, you star,' I said.

'I don't know what I can do about the smell though.'

'I'll get used to it,' I said.

'But what will your teacher say?'

'Oh he stinks anyway,' I said.

Saturday December 28th

Maddy has returned with my geography books all covered – and Edgar.

Edgar is thirteen, going on eighty-six. He's the most elderly teenager you could ever meet. He doesn't go to school any more – he has a tutor now – as the lessons just weren't demanding enough for him. Plus he had to hide a lot from the other pupils.

He is Maddy's only other client. He writes poems – which are a marvellous cure for insomnia. Incredibly though, some have been published in our local paper. But then Maddy is a brilliant agent.

Edgar shook his head at me. 'You must feel terrible.'

'Not now that you're here to cheer me up.'

21

'I expect you are full of inner rage.'

'While you're full of—'

Maddy hastily interrupted me. 'Edgar's got a suggestion for you.'

'At which you'll probably hoot,' said Edgar.

'Probably,' I agreed.

He said, 'I think you should record the act which was so cruelly denied an audience on Christmas Eve and put it on YouTube. This will be both an act of defiance, and—'

'Woah! That's a great idea,' I interrupted before adding two words I never ever thought I'd utter. 'Thanks, Edgar.'

Saturday December 28th

What does a monster eat after he's had his teeth out?
The dentist.

What is the fastest part of a car?
The dashboard.

Quick sample of silly jokes I performed on Poppy's show. Can't wait to tell them again in my new comedy act.

* * *

Sunday December 29th

Just watched back my new comedy act. And I'm awful, possibly even terrible. My timing was off and I didn't bring any energy to the jokes. I merely recited them like someone talking in their sleep.

I think I have lost my sense of humour.

Monday December 30th

2.30 p.m.

Now Maddy has seen my latest performance. At the end she said, 'Maybe you need an audience.'

'But no audience would laugh at me today, would they?'

Maddy got up. 'Louis, you've had a big shock. It would be odd if you were funny after that. So just leave it for a few days. Watch loads of comedy though and soon your humour will return all right. And never forget you are still LOUIS THE LAUGH.'

9.00 p.m.

Just watched all my favourite comedy DVDs – *Porridge*, *Modern Family*, *The Inbetweeners* – and am now reading a book by the amazingly funny P.G. Wodehouse – *Right Ho, Jeeves*. My humour must start to creep back soon.

Tuesday December 31st

Maddy has to go away with her parents for a few days so we had a kiss for New Year's Eve. Then she gave me extra kisses for all the days she'd be away. Having a girlfriend is great.

Wednesday January 1st

2.30 p.m.
Been watching this vlog featuring Noah and Lily. They've become one of the top vloggers and it's not hard to see why.

They may be a couple but they're never yucky. They tell funny stories about themselves, and do wacky challenges. They often interview other celebrity couples too.

Anyway, they were really making me laugh when Mum started peering over my shoulder.

'What is so amusing then?' she asked. I am always keen to educate my parents so I started explaining until Mum cut in.

'But this looks as if it's filmed in someone's extremely messy bedroom.'

'It is. It's coming from Noah's bedroom.'

'And they're not doing very much – just

talking and making silly faces,' went on Mum.

'No, Mum, they're being *real*.'

But Mum shook her head, 'I don't understand why you don't switch it off and go and talk to your brother instead.'

'Now you're just being silly, Mum.'

But afterwards I felt a bit sorry for her. It must be awful being past it.

4.50 p.m.

Poppy rang to wish me Happy New Year and all that rhubarb. Then she said, 'And Louis, I'm really sorry about you being cut from ...'

'Look, it wasn't your fault,' I growled, 'so stop apologising. By the way, every single time I look on the internet there's someone else saying how awesome your show was. I'm dead proud of you. Hey, I sounded almost sincere then didn't I?'

Poppy laughed before saying, 'They have promised that when they repeat my show it will be the full version.'

A tiny hope rose in me. 'Did they say when they'd show it again?'

'No, they didn't,' she admitted.

And promptly died again.

*   *   *

Thursday January 2nd

I was coming out of the shops when a girl from my school shouted at me, 'I didn't go out on Christmas Eve because you said you were going to be on telly. I told all my family as well.' Her voice rose. 'And then you weren't even on it.'

'I had noticed,' I replied. And I thought my head would blow off with disappointment. 'But what happened was ...'

'What happened was you made the whole thing up!' she shouted. 'Well, you wait until next Monday.'

Returning to the Yawn Factory is always grisly. But this time, I know it's really going to make my flesh creep.

Friday January 3rd

11.30 a.m.
No it isn't, as I've had a genius idea.

I was messing about on eBay when I found something.

A guy who lives in the very next road to mine was selling his skateboard – and at what looked like a very reasonable price too. That's when it came to me.

I shan't scuttle into school on Monday, shame

26

dripping off me as I squeal apologies – no, I'll soar in on a skateboard. Of course, it will be instantly confiscated. But that doesn't matter. Because everyone will be talking about me arriving like the coolest pupil who ever walked this earth, while my non-appearance on Poppy's show will be forgotten in seconds.

Now, come on, you must admit that's a brilliant plan.

1.35 p.m.
I am now the proud owner of a skateboard. And if they ever dole out prizes for the world's rustiest one, mine will be up on the winner's podium for certain.

But it doesn't matter – you can't see exactly how rusty it is until you get up really close to it.

6.00 p.m.
Been studying on YouTube all the incredible stunts people do on skateboards. I'm not sure I'll be quite as good as that by Monday. But I'll have a good practice in the park tomorrow. How hard can it be? And don't I already have a certificate up on my bedroom wall proclaiming I can swim 1,000 metres? Swimming and skateboarding – they're sort of similar. In a way. Well they both involve moving don't they?'

27

Saturday January 4th

I think I've just broken my bottom.

And I've got bruises bigger than tennis balls everywhere. And even when I managed to stay upright on my skateboard for five seconds, a one-year-old on a toy bike whizzed right past me.

I hobbled home and got absolutely no sympathy. My parents think I've gone insane spending practically all my Christmas money on it. So anyway, it's now rammed under my bed.

And this is the end of my venture into the world of skateboarding.

Sunday January 5th

Actually it isn't.

Maddy is back and has discovered I do have one great skateboard talent. I am extremely skilled at wearing it.

Maddy's just been watching me strutting about in the park, with the skateboard hanging on my shoulders. I've practised the stance and given it a bit of swagger. 'Now you really look the business,' she said.

So I'll stroll into school first thing tomorrow, a skateboard casually draped over my shoulders and whistling a merry skateboard tune as I do so.

Then before anyone asks me to do anything, a teacher will have whisked the skateboard away and probably give me multiple detentions for daring to have fun on school premises.

But, as Maddy says, my new, cool skateboard image will linger for ages.

Want to know something? I'm almost looking forward to tomorrow now.

Chapter Five

Wearing a Skateboard to School

Monday January 6th

7.20 a.m.
Mum has just burst into my bedroom demanding to know what I'm doing.

I slowly peered up from under my warm, snuggly duvet. 'I'm on Instagram, Mum.'

'I can see that, Louis. But why now?'

Talk about a silly question. But I had to remember that Mum was from another age. So I very patiently explained. 'Young people all over the planet are doing this right now. I mean, check this out. This boy from my school was playing football yesterday when this dog ran up and right there in the middle of the game did this huge poo. Look at the size of it,' I said, pointing excitedly at the screen.

'No thanks,' shuddered Mum.

'But seeing stuff like that really helps wake you up and cheers you up too. Just have a quick peek at ...'

'Did you leave all this stuff on the floor for your father to pick up?' she interrupted

'Or you. I'm not fussy.'

When Mum didn't smile, I added hastily. 'And that's a joke.'

'Louis, stop watching rubbish!' (Rubbish! Has she no idea? It's what's happening in the world today) 'and pick it all up now please.'

While I was still extremely busy doing that, she said, 'And you *will* remember to make your bed today.'

Now that always bugs me, as I'm the only person who ever sleeps in it, so what does it matter if I make my bed or not? And what's it got to do with Mum anyway.

'I know you think I'm being a big nag,' continued Mum (correct), 'but from today your dad's going to be away a lot. Well, he's now enrolled on three extra courses as well as the cookery one.' She smiled suddenly. 'It's wonderful to see your dad his old, enthusiastic self again, isn't it?'

I had to admit it was.

'And he always enjoys talking to you,' she added.

'I can understand that,' I said.

'So will you show an interest in what he's been doing?'

'I'll get him to fill out a questionnaire every night,' I grinned.

'And you might want to have a think about what extra things you can do in the house,' said Mum.

'I might,' I said, without any enthusiasm at all. What with picking up stuff off the floor and making my bed, it seemed to me I'd taken on a crazy amount of new chores already.

8.05 a.m.
Downstairs, Dad was bounding about like a genial Labrador. 'Full cooked breakfast for you, Louis,' he announced.

'You shouldn't have ...' I began.

'It's no trouble,' he said.

'No, I mean I wish you hadn't,' I muttered to myself as I gazed down at the shrivelled up bacon and the oddest looking fried egg I'd ever seen. Dad was starting his cookery lessons not a moment too soon.

As I sat down, Elliot, my midget brother, shook his head gravely. 'When you go into school – well, I wouldn't want to be you today.'

'And I wouldn't want to be you any day.'

'Everyone will go on and on about how you weren't on Poppy's show—'

'And it's still talking,' I interrupted. 'How can you switch it off? Maybe a punch might help.'

Then Elliot started yelling before I'd even touched him.

Dad rushed over. 'What's the matter, Elliot?'

'His potty needs emptying,' I said. 'That's all.'

'Now, lads,' sighed Dad, 'I can hear you two continually sniping at each other and that is not how we talk to each other in this family.'

'Er, it is, actually,' I said.

'No, we look out for each other,' said Dad, 'help one another.'

Then he plonked his hand on my shoulder. 'You might get a few comments when you first walk into school today.'

'Like several billion,' said Elliot.

'But I think your chums' (Chums! My dad must be the last person in the entire universe to still use that word) 'might surprise you, Louis – and be far more understanding about your

33

disappointment than you think.'

It still shocks me how little my parents know of life. Today would undoubtedly be unbelievably ghastly if I didn't have my genius plan.

8.23 a.m.
I waited until everyone had left before sneaking back home. I don't think my parents would understand how vital it is that I take a skateboard to school today. So better they don't know anything about it.

8.41 a.m.
I've sauntered through the school gates, skateboard over my shoulders, and whistling in a cool, mysterious way. Nowhere near as easy as it sounds, actually, but I think I pulled it off all right.

9.05 a.m.
Next, I strutted onto the playground. This dead mouthy guy, Carl, ran over to me, shouting, 'You're such a liar, saying you were on –' He stopped. 'What are you doing with that skateboard?'

I gave a weary smile before saying in a very low and highly mysterious voice, 'Carl, I'm a skater now.'

He stared at me. 'Since when?'

'Oh, a long, long time. But I've only gone public recently. My secret identity is a secret from the world no longer.'

'It's dead rusty,' he said.

I looked shocked. 'This skateboard is an old friend. And I stay loyal to my old friends.'

He was staring at me, kind of disbelieving but fascinated too. Other people started gawping at me and my skateboard too. And no one was mentioning my non-appearance on TV. So that was a result already.

Then a boy yelled out. 'Come on then, give us a demonstration.'

'That's why I brought it with me to show you some of my moves,' I said, while desperately looking around for a teacher. My voice rose, 'Of course, I'm blatantly breaking school rules by doing this. Health and safety rules for a start.'

Then I yelled again only much louder, 'I'm breaking all the health and safety rules here all right!' A whole posse of teachers should have been racing over now – but not a ripple. A crowd of kids had erupted out of nowhere though and were thronging around me.

'Hurry up and do something then,' yelled Carl. I peered round. Never in my life have I been more eager to see a teacher. But wouldn't you just know it, no-one was about.

So in the end I had no choice. Okay, I thought, I'll just do one very brief stunt. Surely, even I can manage that.

I threw back my head, held out my arms, charged forward and then ...

Well let's just say as a way of impressing people, falling on your bum on the school tarmac the very second you get on your skateboard is definitely overrated.

It was only when I was scrambling to my feet, and with mocking laughter raining down on me from all directions, that a teacher FINALLY arrived.

As he led me away I hissed, 'What took you so long? The discipline at this school has really gone downhill.'

4.08 p.m.

Dad was home when I got back. So was Elliot. They both gaped at the skateboard in my hand.

'What on earth ...?' began Dad, his mouth hanging open like a post box.

'It was take your skateboard to school day,' I replied. Then I fled upstairs. Tragic really that people don't realise that looking cool while holding a skateboard takes immense skill. No, they demand you do stuff on it as well.

Well, as a result of their pettiness I shall never be seen with a skateboard again.

Chapter Six

The Walking Germ

Tuesday January 7th

4.00 p.m.

We were queuing up for geography when I casually asked the boy in front of me, 'Is Stinky Coffee Breath back today?'

I thought the boy gave me a very odd look. Then I found out why. Stinky Coffee Breath was standing right behind me. So no, not the best start.

But that's no excuse for Stinky Coffee Breath's behaviour when he saw my geography exercise books. I mean, I thought I was going to have to get him medical help he was frothing at the mouth so much.

Still at least I kept calm as I explained to him that in all the confusion of Christmas my geography books had all accidentally been chucked out. But after I rescued them I was so concerned by their condition I'd even had new covers put on them – I paused here to smile virtuously and allow Stinky Coffee Breath to admire the results.

Instead he yelled at me, 'Do you seriously expect me to mark this?'

I was not the least bit fussed, to be honest. But I did my best to seem concerned. And I was still assuring him that in time my exercise book would probably only have a very slight odour of stinkiness, when he flung it to the ground. Like a madman, he was.

Anyway, I not only had to haul myself from my desk and pick it up – but now I've got to copy everything from my old geography exercise book into a brand new one, which he sent flying across the classroom, and incidentally just missed my head.

Then – after I have done all that work – he'll decide if he's going to mark it or not.

I think his behaviour today has been truly atrocious. But I didn't say anything as his face had turned a deeply unhealthy purple. And I really didn't want him to breathe his last on my account.

I'm just too kind-hearted, aren't I?

4.09 p.m.
Walked home thinking about the end of last year and the start of this one. Some days have been awful. The others have been truly terrible.

And I have turned into one of Life's great flops. But that's not really me. I'm a boy of great comic potential. I'm Louis the Laugh. Need to keep remembering that.

7.20 p.m.
'So how are all your courses going?' I asked Dad, showing a keen interest, exactly as I'd promised Mum.

'They're going really well,' said Dad.

'Great,' I said, thinking that's it. I've done my good deed for the day.

But instead, Dad came and sat down beside me. 'There's one course that's especially interesting,' he said. 'It's called 'Happier Families'.

'I can tell you how to have a happier family,' I replied. 'Give your son a lot more pocket money, starting today.'

'And the tutor, Digby, is extremely encouraging …' Dad went on.

'Digby?' I interrupted. 'I saw a film about someone called Digby once, it was called *Digby, the Biggest Dog in the World*. No relation of his I suppose.'

But Dad wasn't even listening. He was too busy wittering on. 'Digby said this course is really going to challenge us, with tough questions about life today.'

Talking a load of waffle about the meaning of Life is Dad's most favourite thing in the whole world. Especially since he lost his job.

So I jumped up and said. 'That's what I like to hear. Enjoy.'

Yet still Dad rattled on. 'Tough questions like, has living in a world of instant access actually resulted in all of us having weaker social skills – notably within our families and ...'

But I won't bore you any more. I just want you to know that I had to listen to acres and acres of that stuff, and somehow I managed to stay awake and even nod my head occasionally. This must surely count as my good deed for the week. If not the whole month.

8.15 p.m.
Told Maddy about what happened in Coffee Breath's lesson. And I exaggerated it a bit, to make it funnier. But she hardly laughed at all.

41

And when she did, it didn't feel genuine. (And don't forget I am something of an expert on laughing).

You know something else – I sensed she wanted to get off the phone as quickly as possible. You don't think – hey that's too scary to even write. But I will, just here.

You don't think Maddy is cooling off?

Wednesday January 8th

8.05 p.m.
Now Maddy seems to have forgotten she's having a meal round my house.

'I'm going to your house on Thursday?' she murmured like someone in a trance.

'You are still coming, aren't you?' I demanded.

'Of course. It had just slipped my mind for a moment.'

'We picked Thursday night so my parents didn't make such a big deal of it. If it was Friday they'd probably hire a brass band and ...'

'It's okay, Louis, I remember now and I'm looking forward to it.'

'Liar,' I said at once.

She laughed a bit uneasily.

'It's only ...'

'Yeah.'

'No, I've got to go,' and with that she rang off.

8.50 p.m.
Maddy is cooling off, isn't she?

Well you can't blame her, I suppose.

On Christmas Eve I was about to be discovered. A whole world of fame and laughter awaited me. That gave me star quality. All girls like that.

But now, my career has totally stalled. I can't even tell a joke properly. No wonder she always sounds so far away when she's talking to me.

Maddy's already thinking of someone else.

Edgar.

It must be. Only tonight I saw his latest poem in the local paper. And another one is threatened soon.

He is going places all right.

8.52 p.m.
And to think she kissed me three times on New Year's Eve.

Girls are so fickle.

8.54 p.m.
But I will not give up on Maddy.

Tomorrow she will see that despite being rubbish at just about everything right now, I am still worth keeping as a boyfriend.

Thursday January 9th

5.40 p.m.
Wandered into the kitchen where Mum and Dad swooped down on me.

'Here he is,' grinned Dad.

'Bit nervous, I expect,' cooed Mum, 'but excited too.'

'Mum, Maddy has been round here about nine million times before.'

'But not as your girlfriend, coming round to share a meal with us all,' said Mum.

'Don't worry,' said Dad, 'we'll be very welcoming. We'll just say, it's great, Maddy, you're here for an evening of family fun.'

'If you say that she'll probably run away.' Then I added in a helpful way, 'So as not to put you to any bother, it might be best if you kept conversation to an absolute minimum tonight.'

'How about if we just wave at Maddy occasionally?' said Mum.

'Now that could work ...' I began, before I realised Mum wasn't being serious.

A bit hurt now, Mum went on, 'Your dad and I have been working so hard tonight to prepare something special for Maddy.'

'Well, it's mainly been your mum,' said Dad, 'but there is something of me in the cake.'

44

'Errr, which bit?' demanded Elliot, bouncing in. 'Because I'm not eating that.'

'Elliot, that's very rude,' said Mum. In reply Elliot let out a gigantic sneeze, which shot right across the kitchen.

'Elliot, please! Not in here when we're preparing food,' said Dad.

'But no one can control their sneezes,' said Elliot.

'He'll have to eat upstairs,' I said. 'We can't expose Maddy to all his germs.'

'Have you got a cold?' asked Mum.

'Oh yes,' said Elliot proudly. Then he only went and sneezed again. This time, right in my face.

'He's beyond disgusting!' I shouted. 'And now I'm covered in snot. I'll kill him for sure.' Elliot tore out of the kitchen and I made to charge after him.

'No, Louis, calm down and leave this to me,' said Mum firmly.

'There's no way,' I called after her, 'that the Walking Germ is eating with Maddy and me tonight.' Then I asked Dad, 'Have I got any snot on me?'

Dad peered at me. 'Just a little bit above your mouth.'

'Err gross, gross,' I cried, flicking it off.

'Not in the kitchen,' said Dad.

'What does it matter! The whole place is crawling with bugs. And now I've got to wash my face again, when I only washed it last week.'

5.53 p.m.
Heard Mum talking to Elliot in this really quiet voice. Heard him blowing his nose really vigorously too. Then she appeared in my bedroom. 'Elliot's got a really nasty cold,' she said mistaking me for someone who was remotely interested.

'He has agreed,' continued Mum, 'not to eat with us tonight. He'll have something on a tray in his bedroom.'

'Excellent!' I cried. 'You couldn't make him do that that every night could you?'

'But I did say he could come down and say *hello* to Maddy.'

'Why?' I demanded.

'Because he's part of this family too,' said Mum briskly. 'Anyway, Louis, you look very smart.'

'It must be the snot glistening on my face.'

'You're not worried about tonight, are you?'

'No,' I said at once.

'I just thought you seemed a bit uptight.' I was astonished Mum had noticed.

46

And yes, I was uptight. Maddy has sounded so strange recently. Something is definitely wrong. But I'm not giving up.

I'll win her back tonight – somehow.

6.15 p.m.

When Dad called out, 'Maddy's coming down the road' I sped downstairs and opened the front door, just as she came cycling onto my drive on her bike.

And all I did was yell out, 'Hey Maddy!' but the next thing I knew she'd lost control of her bike, and gone spinning off it onto the grass.

I tore over to her. Mum and Dad raced outside too, while Elliot yelled out of the window, 'Is she still alive?'

'I'm all right, I'm fine,' said Maddy at once. But she winced with pain as she said it. And her right ankle was bleeding.

I pulled the bike off her and then slowly helped her up.

Elliot had bounded outside too and very helpfully sneezed twice in Maddy's direction. That's great I thought: she's got a gammy leg and a cold before she's even set foot inside my house. Who knows what ailment she'll get here next.

Leaning heavily on me, Maddy hobbled into

the house.

I helped her into the living room where she lay down on the sofa. Mum put a bandage on her ankle and said it would be best if she rested it for a while. Dad brought her in a cup of tea. After they'd exited she said, 'I bet I look terrible.'

'No you don't,' I said.

'Really?' Right away I knew she wanted me to say some more. You see, I do know a bit about girls.

So with a dead suave smile I said, 'You've put some make-up on, haven't you?'

She nodded.

'I noticed because it makes you look so much better. That's not to say you didn't look great before,' I hastily added. 'But now you look a little bit greater. So keep plastering on the make–up.'

She laughed suddenly and the atmosphere actually relaxed. 'Funny you falling off your bike like that,' I said.

'I haven't done that since I was about two,' she replied.

'It was me stepping outside that seemed to send you tumbling,' I said as a kind of joke.

Suddenly Maddy looked as if she was about to cry.

I crouched down. 'Hey, what's wrong?'

'Everything – and I so didn't want to tell you.'

'Tell me what?'

I was positively alarmed now.

She hesitated. 'Oh Louis, there's no easy way to say this.'

My heart was racing. She really is going to dump me. That's why she lost her balance when she saw me. She knew I'd be upset.

'Just say it Maddy.'

But before she could utter another word Mum and Dad appeared. 'Everything is ready,' said Mum, 'but I can bring it in here to you if you like?'

'It's no trouble,' added Dad.

'No, I'm feeling a bit better now,' said Maddy immediately, struggling to get up, while mouthing at me, 'Tell you later.'

7.10 p.m.

How much longer can this lousy, stinking meal go on for? It's already lasted several trillion years. And how am I expected to eat anything under these conditions?

Maddy's probably been meaning to dump me for ages, but she thought she'd wait until after the Christmas decorations came down. No wonder I feel fantastically miserable. Plus I've got stomach cramps.

And she hasn't even told me yet.

Chapter Seven

Maddy's Shocking News

7.25 p.m.

As soon as the desserts were cleared away Maddy went back to reclining on the sofa. Pacing about a bit I decided to get it over with. 'I know what you're going to tell me.'

Maddy nodded gravely. 'My mum called you, didn't she?' Before I could reply she rushed on. 'She knew how much I dreaded telling you and she thought it might be helpful if she gave you some of the background ...'

I was so shocked and outraged, I stopped pacing and stood over her. 'So you've been discussing this with your mum?'

'Of course.'

'What about your dad?'

'Well, it was his decision really.'

'What!' I exclaimed.

'Although Mum did have a say as well.' Then she added, 'Do you have any idea how awful this is for me?'

For her!

'It's pretty bad for me too,' I said.

'I know.' She looked at me quite sadly. 'And I wish my mum hadn't called you. I knew it wouldn't help.'

'She didn't actually.'

'Was it my dad?'

'No.'

'So how do you know then?'

I frowned down at her. 'You underestimate me, Maddy. I see more than you think. It's obvious, actually. And what have they got against me anyway?'

'Against you?' said Maddy faintly. 'Nothing.'

'Then why are they telling you to dump me?'

Maddy sat up. 'Louis, what are you talking about?'

'What you're talking about – I think.'

She leaned forward. 'My dad's been head-hunted, for what he says is the chance of a lifetime – a new job in America, and we're all moving in ...'

'So you're not finishing with me?' I interrupted.

'No, why would I do that?'

'I don't know. But just to check you're really not.'

'NO! NO! NO!' she shouted.

'What a relief, I'm so happy,' I began. Then I stopped. 'Did you say you're moving to America?'

'In only a few weeks' time as well. On the 10th of February.'

Chapter Eight

Operation Save Maddy

7.25 p.m. (cont'd)

The news slid through me like a knife. I sat down and then got up again. I was speechless with shock – and horror.

'I've known for a few days,' said Maddy, 'but I didn't want to tell you on the phone. I didn't want to tell you at all really.' Her voice fell away for a moment.

'That's why my mum, trying to be helpful, offered to give you a call explaining what a truly, wonderful opportunity this is for my dad. And how moving to America wasn't something they'd decided lightly. I mean, the house probably won't even be sold before we leave, but the firm's paying all the moving fees and is arranging for us to stay at ...' She stopped. 'I haven't known you this quiet, Louis, ever ... Say something.'

'You're not going.'

'And I so don't want to because I'll miss all my friends. Even my school in a sort of way and ... I've become a big fan of you.'

'I've become a big fan of you too,' I said. 'So you're not going anywhere. I mean, we don't live in medieval times. Parents can't make you go with them – especially if you're staying somewhere else.'

'Neither of my sisters are going,' said Maddy.

'That's our solution,' I replied at once.

'They're at university now. And I've been on the phone to both of them for hours and hours, begging them to let me stay with them.'

'So what did they say?' I asked.

'They were very sympathetic, but said it was totally impossible.' Maddy sighed. 'So then I thought of running away. But I don't think I've got the personality for it.'

'No you haven't,' I agreed. 'But, Maddy, you've overlooked the most obvious solution,' I smiled at her triumphantly. 'You can move in here.'

Her eyes widened. 'But won't your parents mind?'

'Oh no, I bet they've always wondered what it

would be like to have a daughter. Now they can find out. Be quite educational for them really.'

'You haven't got any spare rooms though,' said Maddy.

That certainly was a problem. I considered for a moment. 'Maddy, prepare to be humbled by my razor sharp brain.'

'Go on then.'

'You will sleep in my little brother's room.'

'And what about him?'

'He will be sharing with me.'

'He'll never agree to that,' she said.

'You are reckoning without my cunning genius. Somehow I will persuade him. It won't be easy, but I'll do it. And then when he agrees we'll have a totally empty room. After which I'll say to my parents how you are looking to stay on in the area. By the way, I expect your parents will pay a bit of rent for you.'

'I'm sure they will.'

'Well,' I said, 'the extra money should totally swing it. With Dad still out of work ...'

'But you really think you could share a room with your brother?'

I considered for a moment. 'I wouldn't do it for anyone else – but yes I can. We've got to be very clever about this though. So, for a start, I don't want my parents knowing about you being forced to go to America yet. I'd rather wait until there is a free room and then I'll just inform them that you're looking to move in – and why.'

'I think that would be best,' agreed Maddy.

Maddy's dad arrived a few minutes later. Luckily he and my parents only talked briefly – and that was all about Maddy's accident.

It was only when she was getting into the car that her dad turned to me and said, 'I expect Maddy has told you her exciting news.'

'She's told me the news, yes,' I replied in my flattest tones.

'I know she'll stay in contact with you,' he said brightly. 'It really is quite a big adventure for all of us.' And with that he got into the car.

He didn't seem the least bit bothered that he'd totally ruined Maddy's life and mine. His selfishness was truly mind-boggling.

I whispered to Maddy. 'Don't worry, you're not going anywhere.'

'No I'm not, am I?'

Then she took my hand and squeezed it dead hard.

7.40 p.m.
In my bedroom, with my head crammed with plans for saving Maddy, when Mum and Dad piled in. They plonked themselves down on my

bed, looking dead serious.

'Louis,' said Mum, 'we couldn't help noticing that during our meal with Maddy you seemed extremely distracted, as if you had something on your mind.'

Well of course I had. I was convinced Maddy was about to dump me.

'So we just wondered,' said Dad, 'if something was bothering you.'

I was about to say, 'No, clear off,' when an idea formed.

So instead I swallowed hard. 'Actually, there is something.'

Mum and Dad immediately leaned forward.

'Tell us in your own time,' said Dad.

'Well, it's Elliot.' I lowered my voice. 'How ill is he?'

'He's not ill at all,' said Mum. 'He's only got a feverish cold.'

'But you don't think you should ring the doctor?' I asked.

'Whatever for?' Mum demanded.

'Just to be completely certain,' I said.

Mum was gaping at me as if I'd just started babbling in a new language.

'I know it seems as if Elliot and I are always arguing,' I went on.

'It really does,' said Mum.

'But he and I – we do talk a lot too.' Warming to my new role as Elliot's caring older brother I continued, 'I'm just glad the little fella's going to be all right.'

There was a truly stunned silence for a moment.

Dad sprang to his feet. All at once he seemed ten years younger. 'You know I always suspected that underneath all the … the …'

'Friendly banter,' I suggested.

Dad nodded. 'That you and you brother did genuinely care about each other. I don't suppose …'

'What Dad?' I asked.

'That you'd like to take a hot drink up to Elliot.'

'Dad,' I said with every ounce of sincerity I could muster, 'I'd so like that.'

'Operation Save Maddy' has begun.

8.50 p.m.

The second I shuffled in with his hot drink, Elliot looked wary.

'So how are you feeling?' I asked.

'What's it to you?'

'Hey, don't be like that,' I said, putting the drink down and then making as if to ruffle his hair in a matey sort of way.

'Don't hit me,' he cried.

'As if I would, especially when I've been so worried about you.'

At that moment Elliot released a gigantic sneeze, which exploded, over his bed and onto my hand. He immediately started to laugh as globules of snot now gleamed on my right hand.

'Ha, ha,' I said, flicking the snot on to his carpet. 'You got me there, good shot.' I even managed to twist my face into a smile.

'Anyway,' I said, 'I hope you'll be feeling better soon because it's so quiet downstairs without you.'

Elliot glared at me suspiciously. 'Why are you acting all weird?'

'I'm not.'

'Yes you are!' he shouted. 'Now get out, as you're really scaring me. Go on, get out!'

This was going to be harder than I thought.

Chapter Nine

My Cunning Genius

Friday January 10th

5.10 p.m.
Just spent twenty minutes in my little brother's bedroom. Now I feel as if someone has stamped on my nose.

I mean, Mum thinks *my* bedroom smells. But mine are just normal boy stinks. Elliot's room reeks of dried farts, dirty feet and sick. And those are only the good smells.

Apart from the stink, the whole time he was talking to me Elliot lay picking his nose. But I didn't even let that put me off. The things I do for my girlfriend.

'Elliot, how are you feeling?' I asked, dripping with fake concern.

'Terrible.'

I put on my saddest face. 'I'm sorry about that. Would you like me to get you a drink or something to eat – or maybe I could blow your nose for you. That last one is a joke, by the way.'

Elliot peered at me very suspiciously. 'Why are you being like this?'

'Like what?'

'Like you're bothered about me.'

'Because I am.'

Elliot gave a snort of laughter.

'No, I mean, I'm your big brother. You look up to me ...'

That made Elliot laugh so hard he had a coughing fit.

'No honestly, I care about you. And to prove it you can borrow anything of mine you like to brighten up your dull existence.'

A little gleam came into Elliot's eyes. 'Can I borrow your iPhone?'

'You want to borrow my iPhone?' I said in a low, trembling voice. Elliot wasn't allowed one yet. He only had a tablet. He was intensely annoyed about this, claiming he was the only boy in his year not to have an iPhone.

'Yeah, that's what I really want.'

'Anything else you'd rather have instead?' I asked hopefully.

'No, I only want to borrow your iPhone. Nothing else.'

Then somehow – and don't ask me how I did it – in a low, trembling voice I gasped, 'All right.'

'Really?' Elliot was astonished.

'You're my little brother – nothing's too much trouble for you. So yeah, you can borrow it. Only for tonight, though.'

'Can I have it now?'

'Yeah. Sure. I know you'll look after it.'

'Oh I will,' said Elliot.

I returned with it, just as Dad looked in. 'Louis's letting me borrow his iPhone,' Elliot chimed excitedly.

'Only for a very little while today,' I cried.

'Well that's so kind of you, Louis,' said Dad.

'What are brothers for?' I murmured.

Outside I was sweaty and red-faced, both with the stench and the thought of Elliot's fat, clumsy hands anywhere near my iPhone.

5.15 p.m.

Downstairs in the kitchen Dad was still exclaiming about my generosity.

'But do you know what's really inspired me?'

'No, tell me Dad.'

'That you and Elliot are working together at last.'

'We really are,' I assured him.

'And thinking like a team,' Dad went on.

'Oh definitely.'

'Family life,' said Dad, 'becomes really special when we put aside all our petty squabbles — which are inevitable — and focus instead on what unites us. That's what's truly important. The bond we share.'

I pretended to be thinking deeply about this bilge before saying slowly. 'I think you're right, Dad. And you know what, I'm going to try and remember what you said.'

Dad beamed at me. 'By the way, I did enjoy seeing Maddy yesterday. Will you tell her she's welcome here anytime?'

'Anytime,' I repeated excitedly. 'And can she stay as long as she likes?'

'But of course,' said Dad. 'I want Maddy to feel really at home here.'

Now I was beaming too.

5.45 p.m.

Just told Maddy exactly what Dad had said. 'But did he mean I could stay with you for months and months. Years even? He might not want me for all that time.'

'What you're forgetting, Maddy,' I replied, 'is that you grow on people.'

'Oh yes,' she agreed. 'I was forgetting that.'

Saturday January 11th

9.50 p.m.
Back in my brother's room. This time I nearly passed out from the stench – and from being so revoltingly nice to him. He's got to spend another morning in bed. And he only wants to borrow my iPhone AGAIN.

Somehow I say, through clenched teeth, 'Of course, young sir, you can borrow it one last time.'

Elliot snatches my iPhone from me before asking. 'Are you having a nervous breakdown?'

'Ha, ha,' I laugh merrily.

'I don't mind if you are,' he says. 'In fact, I prefer you when you're crazy.'

4.00 p.m.
I've finally got my iPhone back. Elliot has changed my ring tone. And he has loaded on a whole load of his rubbish games. And he's deleted tons of my stuff.

He's not going anywhere near my iPhone again.

EVER.

Thank goodness I move on to Phase Two of 'Operation Save Maddy' tomorrow.

Sunday January 13th

10.05 a.m.

Bounced into Elliot's room. 'So how are you feeling, buddy?'

He was propped up in bed. 'You're still weird then,' he said, but for the first time he was sort of smiling at me too. 'They say I'm well enough to go back to school tomorrow.'

'What a shame.' Then dredging up a long, distant memory I went on. 'Do you remember at our old house how we used to go off on our bikes and have adventures, just you and me?'

'Yeah,' he said cautiously.

'And we'd tear through the woods acting as if a flesh-eating ghost was chasing after us.'

'You told me,' Elliot continued, 'that the world was going to be taken over by flesh-eating ghosts, and I got so frightened I fell off my bike.'

'Happy memories. Well I want us to have more adventures like that.'

'But we don't live anywhere near those woods anymore,' said Elliot.

'So we'll have different, better adventures! I

thought we'd start ...' I paused. 'Well, it's not right you should be stuck in this pokey little room, so I'm inviting you to move into my bigger bedroom.'

'And where will you be?' asked Elliot.

'I'll be there too, of course.'

'So we'll both be in your bedroom together?'

'Yeah, won't that be a riot?' I said.

'What will we do in there?'

'We'll hang out – and sleep of course – and ...'

'Both in your bed?'

'Yeah, it's big enough. Later we might move in a new bed, but for now ...'

I stopped. Elliot was laughing and coughing but mainly laughing.

'What's so funny?' I demanded.

'You,' he said.

'Well I'm hurt,' I muttered. 'I make you an offer to share my room ...'

'What are you up to?' interrupted Elliot, now sitting up in bed with his arms folded. 'Tell me the truth or get out.'

Chapter Ten

Bribery Rules

10.05 a.m. (cont'd)

I hesitated. Then I decided I had no option. So I told him about Maddy being forced to move zillions of miles away because of her selfish parents.

He listened to me with bright-eyed attentiveness. 'So Maddy will have my room.'

'Yeah, that's right.'

'And what do I get?' he demanded.

'The undiluted pleasure of my company …'

'What else?' he interrupted.

'What else?' I laughed. 'Isn't that enough?'

'Nowhere near,' said Elliot firmly. 'But I will do it if you let me borrow your iPhone permanently

– well, until I get my own one.'

I drew in my breath with a horrified whoosh. Then I could only make little gulping noises. Finally I said, 'No, that's totally out of the question.' I added quietly, 'But you can borrow my trampoline.'

'I do anyway.'

'All right, you can legally borrow my trampoline – and my bike as well.'

Elliot has always envied my bike. As he considered this, I waited hopefully.

Then he gave his verdict. 'Sharing a bike is not enough for giving up a bedroom. Sharing an iPhone is.'

'I'm the one who makes the jokes,' I said. After all the damage Elliot had inflicted on my iPhone in just 24 hours, the thought of him – NO, I'd be very, very insane to agree to that.

So I said firmly, 'That's too much.'

'Then I stay in my bedroom,' said Elliot. 'Leave quietly will you? I think I'll have a little nap now.'

'I offered to be a proper big brother to you,' I began indignantly. Elliot's only reply was to snore loudly.

I'm now madly thinking what to do.

*   *   *

11.00 a.m.

Edgar has just called round. 'I shan't stay long,' he announced.

'Excellent,' I replied.

'You are the least intellectual person I know,' he said, 'but still, congratulations are in order from me. Arranging for Maddy to move into your house is a remarkable ...'

'Keep your voice down. I'm still working on my parents.'

'Of course, sorry. It's just I can't imagine anything worse than Maddy moving to America. They really broke the mould with her, didn't they?'

On that point anyway, Edgar and I could agree.

After he'd gone I reached a shocking conclusion. I've been a total idiot. And who'd have thought that Edgar, of all people, would bring me to my senses? How could I have forgotten that there are a tiny number of things that are even more important than my iPhone.

Well just the one really.

11.30 a.m.

I tore back upstairs. Elliot was dressed now and energetically brushing his hair.

'All right, you can borrow my iPhone until you

69

get one of your own,' I said, and then I collapsed on to a chair.

'Yes!' cried Elliot, flinging the hairbrush on to the floor in his excitement.

'I know you won't change the settings without my permission, or use it when you're going to the loo or picking your nose—'

'You must really like her,' he interrupted before adding, 'Can I use all your other stuff too whenever I feel like it?'

He was so pushing it now, but I just said. 'Well, you'll be in my bedroom all the time, so I can hardly stop you.'

A big smile was spreading across Elliot's face. 'Actually it won't be your bedroom anymore, will it? It will be *our* bedroom.'

'That's right,' I said faintly. 'Our bedroom now.'

'And Mum and Dad won't mind?' he asked.

'Why should they? You and I are only messing up one room rather than two, which will save them hours of work for a start. Plus they get to have the daughter they've always wanted. But we've got to tell them in the right way,' I added, 'so not a word about Maddy yet. Instead, you'll have to say you really look up to me.'

Elliot made loud throwing up noises.

'In fact, you kind of hero worship me and

that's why you want to spend more time with me.'

'Mum and Dad will never ever believe that,' said Elliot.

'You've got to make them believe it – just think of my iPhone while you're talking to them.'

'And when do we tell them?'

'Later tonight,' I said, 'when Mum gets back.' Even on a Sunday Mum was sometimes called out on estate agency business. I stretched out my hand. 'Do we have a deal?'

'Deal,' said Elliot shaking my hand very vigorously.

6.30 p.m.
'Hey, we've got a bit of news for you,' I said to Mum and Dad. They were both in the kitchen.

'What have you two been up to now then?' asked Dad.

'Elliot's asked me if he could move into my bedroom,' I said 'and I have agreed to … his request.' And then, well you know those moments when they cut to someone on the TV news or something and they don't realise they're on air and so just stare blankly ahead of them. Well that's exactly how my parents looked, as if we'd temporarily lost our connection with them. I suppose that's what shock does to you.

71

They gaped at us. Then gaped some more. 'We certainly weren't expecting that,' said Mum at last.

'I can see that,' I said laughing.

Elliot laughed too before adding, 'I'd like to move my stuff into Louis's room tonight.'

'But why ...?' Mum struggled to finish her sentence. 'Why do you want to move in together?'

I had my answer ready. 'Well it was something Dad said actually.'

'Tell us more,' said Mum, glancing over at Dad as she said this.

'You remember, Dad,' I said, 'how you suggested that Elliot and I should start thinking like a team?'

'Yes ...' he began cautiously.

'Well, you explained it so well that you truly inspired me. And lately – well, you've probably noticed – I've been spending much more time with Elliot. Of course, years ago he and I used to hang out together all the time going off on our bikes ...'

'Escaping from flesh-eating ghosts,' joined in Elliot, 'who wanted nothing less than world domination.'

'And now, thanks to Dad, we're best buddies all over again,' I said. 'Cheers, Dad. We owe you.'

'But I still don't understand why you want to

move in together?' persisted Mum. I knew she'd be the tricky one.

I sighed heavily. 'Okay, Elliot's got problems.'

'What sort of problems?' demanded Mum at once.

'Boys stuff,' I said. 'The kind you need big brothers for.'

'And having Louis to talk about them day and night,' said Elliot, 'is going to help me so much. I really look up to him, actually. He's the best brother you could wish for.'

'Now I know I'm dreaming,' said Mum.

Dad was looking a bit glassy-eyed too but smiling as well.

'So we'll start moving in together right now,' I said. And before either of them could reply we tore upstairs.

6.45 p.m.

Elliot is tearing in and out of my room, scattering his stuff around as he does so. Mum is calling after him, 'Elliot, don't unpack everything now. Look on tonight as a sleepover.'

But this can't be a one-night arrangement. Elliot has to actually move out. So, showing quite extraordinary bravery I say, 'It's all right, Elliot can bring everything in now.'

6.51 p.m.

Mum and Dad are standing on the landing, watching Elliot and me diving about, in a highly puzzled sort of way. 'What exactly did you say to Louis?' Mum is asking Dad.

'Not very much really, but it's obviously made a big impact,' said Dad.

'Well, next perhaps you can persuade him to actually do some homework,' said Mum.

'I'll do my best,' laughed Dad. 'But for now, let's just enjoy our boys acting as a team.' He is chuffed to bits with himself.

6.56 p.m.

Elliot is darting about my bedroom, slapping up stickers of dinosaurs EVERYWHERE.

'I know you are very excited, due to the fact you are,' I said. 'But do you have to put up quite so many pictures of dinosaurs? One or two is fine. But a thousand is overdoing it a bit.'

He totally ignored me.

7.01 p.m.

And now he has bunged up a gigantic poster of the lamest band ever. So every morning when I wake up I'll have their inane grins to greet me.

*   *   *

74

7.20 p.m.
Elliot's still unpacking. And I cannot believe the amount of tat he has brought, including all his toys from when he was even more immature than he is now. This is a bedroom not a junk shop. It's filling up so fast that I doubt there'll be room for me in it soon.

Too depressed to write any more.

7.25 p.m.
What do you call a donkey with three legs?
  A wonkey.

There are times when only a very silly joke keeps you sane. So here's a couple more.

Why did the baby strawberry cry?
Because his parents were in a jam.

What happened to the couple who met in a revolving door?
They're still going round together.

7.40 p.m.
Maddy's just rung to ask how things are going.

'Well, I'm about to share my bed with a grubby, farty, totally annoying little squirt, with death ray bad breath, so not brilliant to be honest.'

'You can't do this,' said Maddy.

I took a deep breath. 'I really can.'

'Louis,' said Maddy. 'You are truly incredible.'

After hearing Maddy say that I felt as if I could share my bedroom with Elliot for ten years and not even care.

'By the way, get ready to move into my house on Tuesday.'

'Tuesday!' she echoed.

'Oh yeah, things are about to move extremely fast,' I said.

Chapter Eleven

Maddy Moves In

Monday January 18th

7.25 a.m.
My brother's stale, stinky breath woke me up.

He lay sprawled across 99 per cent of my bed with his mouth wide open. No wonder I started coughing.

'Can't you cough more quietly?' demanded Elliot. 'You woke me up. And do you always snore?'

'Only when I'm asleep.'

'And your feet really stink. And your bottom.' Then he started giggling insanely.

I closed my eyes. Every morning now I'll wake

up to cheery conversations like this.

'When's Maddy moving into my bedroom?' he asked.

My eyes shot open. 'Sssh.'

'Do you think she's super hot?'

I glared over at him. 'Don't ever ask me questions like that.'

'You can tell me, now we're sharing a room. Is she the full package?'

I sat up in bed. 'If you don't shut up I'll sit on your head.'

'You wouldn't dare.'

'Say one more thing about Maddy ...'

'I'll say what I want. This is my room now too. And you can't stop me.'

I was about to demonstrate how I could stop him when the bedroom door opened. There were Mum and Dad peering in at us, all wide-eyed.

'Here they are, our new best buds,' said Dad. 'So what's it been like bunking up together boys?'

'We thought we could hear raised voices,' said Mum.

'No, just early morning banter,' I replied quickly.

Mum still looked sceptical. 'We're rather thrown by this sudden change in your behaviour ...'

'I wouldn't say thrown exactly,' interrupted

Dad.

'I would,' said Mum.

I was about to answer when Elliot said softly, 'Louis's been such a big help to me. In fact, I just don't know what I'd do without it – him,' he quickly corrected himself.

Then Mum said, 'Elliot, I'm really pleased you feel you can open up to Louis. What I don't understand is why you both want to squash in here.'

'They're chilling together,' interrupted Dad, 'so let's just enjoy that remarkable phenomenon, shall we? Now, who's going to use the bathroom first?'

'You may, Elliot,' I said ultra politely.

'Thank you so much,' replied Elliot equally politely. 'But you must use the bathroom first tomorrow, Louis.'

'Are these really our sons?' Mum asked Dad.

He chuckled, 'We'd better get used to this new caring vibe.'

Mum and Elliot left. Dad hovered in the doorway. 'I emailed Digby about how you and Elliot are spending more time together and he was incredibly interested. Digby's my tutor on the Happier Families course.'

'I know who he is,' I murmured. I should do. Dad mentions him at least once an hour.

'Well, I've invited him round to have a meal with us tomorrow night. I expect he'll want to hear more about the great things that are happening in this house.'

'I expect so,' I murmured while my brain whirled speedily. I'd planned to move Maddy in tomorrow night. But I still could. A guest in the house might even make it easier. There'll be so much going on my parents would probably hardly even notice. Well not until Maddy was safely settled in anyway. Yeah, that could work well.

So I said. 'Sure, I'll give Digby the low-down on how Elliot and I are a team again. No problem.'

5.10 p.m.
I switched on *Blue Peter*, and there was Poppy. I couldn't believe it. She performed three magic tricks at once. Now I'd seen her do this before, but never as well as she did it this time.

Then the presenters said they had 'a big surprise' for Poppy. Two super fans wanted to send her a message. 'These fans,' the presenters trilled on, 'also happen to be big vlogging stars.'

And there, grinning away were Noah and Lily. 'Poppy you are soooo spectacularly brilliant,' said Noah.

'And we so admire the way,' said Lily, 'you

80

haven't let being in a wheelchair stop you from following your dream of being a magician.'

Poppy could only splutter, 'This is awesome,' over and over.

And I'd have been exactly the same. The idea of Noah and Lily even knowing who I was – let alone saying they admired me – seemed about as likely as me scoring the winning goal in a World Cup final.

Afterwards I did think of sending Poppy a text to say how excellent she'd been. But she's left me so far behind in the show business firmament I decided she'd only think I was being creepy.

5.16 p.m.
Maddy rang and immediately asked. 'Did you see Poppy on ...?'

'I sure did. She's even better than when we saw her. And then to have Noah and Lily spout about her. Noah and Lily!'

'It'll be your turn next,' said Maddy.

'Of course it will,' I quickly agreed. 'I've been practising telling jokes on my phone. And I'm better than I was but still not good enough.'

'But you do have very high standards,' Maddy added. 'I've nearly finished my packing. Am I still moving in tomorrow?'

'Definitely.'

'I can't believe how swiftly you've sorted all this out.'

And there was real admiration in Maddy's voice.

'The only bit I'm dreading,' she continued, 'is actually telling my parents that I'm moving out.'

'Always remember, you have a perfect right not to go with them. The law says that.'

'Does it?'

'Well I haven't checked all the details, but I bet it does. There's bound to be a ruling that parents can only force you to move hundreds of miles away if you haven't got somewhere else to go. But you so have. And the fact we're doing it now gives them a chance to get used to you moving out before they leave. So we're being very humane really.'

6.20 p.m.

Dad's been learning how to make a Victoria sponge cake. Today he gave us a taster. It was so heavy it was like eating cold mashed potatoes.

He gave a ghost of a smile as he said. 'It seems my capacity to mess up even simple cooking is limitless.'

'Oh no ...' began Mum.

'It could have been worse,' I said kindly.

'How?' demanded Elliot.

Tuesday January 14th (Maddy's moving-in day)

6.50 a.m.
Elliot woke me up before six o'clock this morning asking inane questions. 'You might as well answer me,' he said, 'as I'm going to be here every morning now.'

'That does not make me feel better,' I said.

Then Elliot asked me if he could borrow one of my computer games. I'll be lucky if I have any possessions left soon.

7.50 a.m.
Mum's just caught Elliot on my iPhone.

'Oh, I don't think you should be using Louis's —'

'It's all right,' interrupted Elliot, 'Louis lets me borrow it now. I think he wants to make up for being such a rubbish brother.'

Mum immediately called me downstairs. And when I confirmed Elliot's story what she'd been told – well, her eyebrows were bouncing off the ceiling. It was just lucky her work rang and she had to go charging off immediately.

4.05 p.m.
Maddy's parents still don't know about her

change of address. And now she thinks it might be best if she left them a note. She's sent me a copy of it. It says:

Dear Mum and Dad,
The news that you are moving away is very disappointing and I will miss you a lot. You are probably wondering why I wrote I will miss you. The reason is, I will not be going with you.
But do not worry. I am not running away to lead the life of a fugitive. I shall be staying with Louis and his family. They say you may drop round at any time and I sincerely hope you will.
I meant to say this to you face to face but the atmosphere at home is as thick as treacle.
Thank you for letting me air my views and reading this. I will always remember you.
With mainly fond memories,
Maddy
P.S. I am only taking two bags with me now. Perhaps you would be kind enough to bring over the rest of my luggage at a time convenient to you.

I called her and said. 'That was brilliant, even brought a tear to my eye.'

And now I'm off to escort Maddy to her new home.

5.00 p.m.

Maddy's parents are away doing the weekly shop, so it's a perfect moment for her to slip away.

She was waiting for me with two small packed bags. 'These are my necessities,' she began, and then she looked at me. 'I should be nervous, but right now I'm just ridiculously excited. I'm living my life for the first time.'

'And it's all going to be so brilliant,' I said.

Maddy slipped her letter on to the kitchen table. 'They'll come in with all the shopping and see this waiting for them.'

'Bit of a surprise,' I said.

'Oh yes, they don't suspect a thing. I expect they'll miss me now and again.'

'Bound to.' I paused for a second. 'I'm trying to feel sad for them, but I can't. After all, it's their extreme selfishness which has caused all this.'

Maddy nodded. 'And they really can visit anytime they want?'

'Oh sure,' I said at once.

'So it's the perfect solution really.' Then she unexpectedly gave me a little hug.

We left, with Maddy carrying one bag, me the other.

'I gave the chauffeur the afternoon off, I'm

afraid,' I said.

'It's all right, I'll walk just this once,' she grinned.

5.40 p.m.

When we arrived at my house I said, 'I'll show you to your room. But I should warn you, we gave the cleaner the afternoon off too. In fact the only staff we have left is a madman who claims he's my dad.'

Upstairs Elliot shot out of our bedroom. He gawped at us in shocked silence, as if he couldn't believe Maddy really was moving in. Then he hissed at me. 'Have you just dropped one?' before giggling loudly and running off.

'Bye, Elliot. Don't hurry back,' I said.

He was off to have his tea at a friend's house.

I ushered Maddy into her new bedroom. I felt oddly shy for a moment. I think she did too as we both just looked at each other.

'Okay, well I expect you'd like to settle in and freshen up.' I never quite know what that means but Mum always says that to guests. 'And do what you like in here. It's your bedroom now. Not too small or smelly is it?'

'No, not at all,' said Maddy at once. She grinned, 'Nice pad.'

I grinned back. 'Now, when you want to come

downstairs, there's no need to put on a false beard or anything, as I'm going to totally clear it with Dad about you staying here right now.'

I sped downstairs. Dad was in the kitchen frowning. 'Digby will be here soon and there's no sign of your mum. I'm not sure if I should start the meal myself or not.'

Knowing Dad's culinary skills I would say definitely not. But I just smiled sympathetically.

'I don't suppose,' asked Dad, 'you know anything about lamb cutlets?'

'I know I like eating them – but that's all really.' Then I went on breezily, 'By the way, Dad, Maddy's here. She's come to stay for a while.'

'Another person to make faces about my cooking, I suppose. But that's fine, we've plenty and it'll be good to have another female round the table.'

'That's what I thought,' I said. Then I said slowly and significantly. 'Maddy's upstairs at the moment, and she's settling in.'

'She's always welcome,' said Dad absently.

'Really?' I looked at him.

'Yes of course.'

'Well, thanks, Dad,' I said, 'we appreciate that.'

'I don't suppose,' he asked suddenly, 'Maddy

knows anything about cooking lamb cutlets?'

'I'll go and ask her now. I know she's looking forward to staying here until she finishes her GCSE exams,' I said this last sentence just as Dad's mobile was going off. But before he sprang to answer it, distracted he nodded, 'Okay, sure,' which means it's all settled, doesn't it?

I couldn't wait to tell Maddy.

Upstairs I bounced in; she'd already unpacked most of her stuff. 'It's okay, Maddy, Dad said you're always welcome here. And I asked if you could stay just until you'd finished your GCSE exams – I didn't want to push it too much – and right away he said, 'Yes!'

'But that's so kind of him.'

'He has his good moments,' I conceded.

'And did he have any questions?'

'Just the one,' I replied. 'Do you know anything about lamb cutlets?'

6.01 p.m.
Maddy's in the kitchen taking charge. She also said thank you to Dad for letting her stay. 'I'm so grateful …' she began.

'No, Maddy,' he replied. 'I'm the one who's grateful. You've saved the day.' Then Dad asked her if she would teach him how to cook the lamb.

They're getting on so well.

Things really couldn't be working out better.

6.10 p.m.
Digby's swanned in. Funny, I'd pictured him as a very tall, heavily bearded guy in a black polo neck. Instead, he's smallish but with a huge moon face and an enormous toothy grin. He was dressed like a mad parrot in a bright orange top and even brighter yellow trousers.

He said to me, 'I'm so looking forward to hearing all about you.' He speaks really slowly and softly, as if he's trying to hypnotise you.

'My wife should be back any moment,' apologised Dad. 'But she's had a bit of a crisis at work today. Another one – so I'm afraid the meal is something of a work in progress.'

'Ah, but we're all works in progress,' said Digby with a smile.

'That's so true,' said Dad. 'I certainly know I am.' He and Digby had a big laugh then.

Dad went on. 'But I have been lucky enough to have the help of Maddy, who I think I can see peeping round the corner. Yes, come in Maddy, and take a bow. You have saved the meal tonight.'

So Maddy stepped forward, smiling shyly. 'Now, Maddy is my son's girlfriend. But we also see her as very much one of the family.'

This was more than I'd dared hope. Maddy hasn't even been here an hour yet and already Dad's saying she's one of the family.

Chapter Twelve

Total Confusion

6.20 p.m.

I knew Maddy's parents would call round at
some time. In fact I'd been expecting them. So
when I opened the door and saw them I'd already
decided on my tactics. I'd be incredibly cheerful
and incredibly firm.

So I said. 'Hey, good of you to drop by. Turned
cold again, hasn't it?'

'Is Maddy here?' demanded her dad.

'Yeah, that's exactly where she is.'

'She left us this note,' said Maddy's mum,
sounding both indignant and upset.

'I know, I saw it. Very well written, I thought.'

Maddy's dad frowned heavily. 'We need to see

her.'

'What, now?' I asked.

His voice rose. 'Yes, now!'

'Of course,' I said, still all sunny confidence. 'Come in and make yourselves at home.' But as I didn't want them venturing too far I added, 'In the doorway.'

I sped off and whispered something to Maddy in the kitchen. She whispered something back, and then I raced off to Maddy's parents again.

'Sorry, Maddy is very busy right now. But she sends you her very best wishes and says call round again any time you want. We can fit in with your plans. Doing anything special this evening?' I added conversationally.

They didn't answer. Instead, like two sleepwalkers they kind of floated to the door. 'Don't be strangers, now,' I called after them. I really do have a massive talent for diplomacy.

7.05 p.m.

When I'd asked Maddy's parents to call round anytime I hadn't meant two minutes after their last visit.

But my smile didn't flicker.

'Hey, back again already. So how can I help this time?'

No answer at first. Then I heard a very

strange noise, like a faraway rumble of thunder. Only it was coming from Maddy's dad.

'Are you telling us,' asked Maddy's mum, speaking very slowly, for some reason, 'that Maddy has moved in here with your parents' consent?'

'That's right.' Then, as I like to be strictly accurate about these things I added. 'Well, Mum doesn't know yet. But my dad agreed right away. In fact, he said tonight that Maddy can stay here with us until she's finished her GCSEs.'

Maddy's mum let out a sharp howl of shock.

'Oh don't worry, I'm sure he won't chuck her out when she's sixteen either,' I went on quickly. 'In fact, he also said that she's like one of the family and has put her to work in the kitchen already,' I smiled reassuringly. 'I think he's always wanted a daughter, actually. And now he's got one. Hope that's put your minds at ease.'

Maddy's dad didn't look as if his mind had been put at ease. In fact he more closely resembled someone who was about to explode. There really was no pleasing some people. I tell you, the sooner this pair were shipped off to America the better. But I just said in a kindly way, 'There's no rush about bringing over the rest of Maddy's stuff. Any time in the next few ...'

'Get Maddy here now!' barked her dad.

'And we want a word with your father too!' Maddy's mum practically screamed at me.

They really were pushing it tonight.

But I kept my cool.

'Well, I'll see if they can spare you a couple of minutes as you're so insistent.' Then I chugged off and returned with them both. I wasn't surprised Maddy was a bit cross. I thought her parents had really let themselves down tonight. But Dad beamed at them.

'Hi there. We've got Maddy working away in the kitchen.'

'So we've heard,' said Maddy's dad so fiercely, that Dad stepped back from him.

'Is everything all right?' Dad quavered.

Both of Maddy's parents spluttered a bit here. 'We didn't know anything about Maddy coming here,' said Maddy's Mum.

'Yes you did,' Maddy interrupted. 'I wrote you a note.'

'Which explains everything,' I added.

'But I expect you didn't find it,' offered Dad.

'Oh no, we found it,' said Maddy's mum.

'But you thought she should have told you in person?' said Dad.

'It's not just that,' began Maddy's mum.

'Oh isn't it?' said Dad. And it was hard to say who looked more confused now. Then Dad spotted Digby hovering in the doorway, ears flapping away. 'May I introduce you to ...' began Dad.

But Maddy's dad totally ignored Digby and roared. 'You should have come round and seen us first.'

'I should?' squeaked Dad.

'Not that we would have ever agreed to this anyway,' said Maddy's mum, her whole body shaking with emotion.

'Of course we wouldn't,' thundered her dad.

Dad was looking more and more bewildered. 'I'm sorry but I'm not completely sure what the problem is.'

'You're not completely sure what the problem is,' echoed Maddy's dad incredulously.

And then Mum arrived. 'Sorry to be so late. Why are ...?'

'Did you know about this?' interrupted Maddy's mum rudely.

'Know about what?' asked Mum.

'About allowing Maddy to live here with you,' said her mum, 'when we emigrate to America?'

'What?' Mum practically shrieked.

'Don't worry, Mum,' I explained. 'Maddy's just moved into Elliot's old room, that's all. And you said you always wanted a daughter, didn't you?'

Here, Maddy smiled ever so sweetly at Mum.

But Mum was looking daggers at Dad. 'You haven't honestly agreed to this, have you?'

'Tell her, Dad! Tell her what you told me,' I prompted. 'That Maddy can stay here until she finishes her GCSEs.'

That's when Dad shied back like a startled horse. He also swallowed three, maybe even four times and still couldn't manage to speak.

Finally Digby stepped forward. 'May I introduce myself? I'm Digby, lecturer, happiness coach and family mediation expert. You may have heard me on the local radio. I'm a very regular contributor.' Everyone except Dad stared blankly at him. 'As a stranger in these parts, might I suggest we all sit down together to sort this out? And I'm going to ask that we have only one rule – everyone's point of view is of value.'

And then ...

LOUSY STINKING LIFE

7.20 p.m.

Sorry about that.

No I'm not, actually.

In fact, I'm going to write it again.

LOUSY STINKING LIFE, because I'm very angry, and you will be too when you hear what happened next.

We all crowded into our living room. Digby had placed himself right in the centre and had us all doing deep breathing exercises, so we could breathe in feelings of calm and peace. 'Hippy dippy nonsense,' muttered Maddy's dad.

'Now, after this,' said Digby 'I sometimes ask people to lie on the floor.' Maddy's dad gave a low, warning growl. 'But I think we've all found a core of peace and tranquillity,' said Digby quickly. 'So who would like to start our healing conversation?'

Maddy's parents were off telling my relics all about their move to America. They totally ignored Maddy and me (and Digby actually).

Finally Digby piped up. 'Maybe it's time to hear from the young people now,' just as if Maddy and I were leprechauns or something.

I said quickly, 'No offence to Maddy's mum and dad and I'm sure she will miss you from time to time – but Maddy wants to live here with us now. And I can't see any problem with that, as she's clean and funny and would be a favourite in any family. Plus, I really like having her around.'

'Thanks, Louis,' said Maddy softly.

I turned to Dad. 'You'll love having Maddy here. I mean, look how she helped you out tonight. And she's a very helpful person – as I know. And, Mum,' I turned my attention on to her, 'you'd have a daughter, which you've always wanted, and during her most interesting years too. So I'd say its all sorted.'

Then I paused hopefully. And neither set of parents spoke at first. But I noticed my mum and dad were shaking. Then I saw Maddy's parents were too. At first I thought they were crying.

But no, they were laughing. All four of them. And very soon they were laughing out loud.

But for once I hadn't been telling jokes. So what was so hilarious?

Still smiling away, Maddy's mum stood up and said. 'I think it's best if we continue this conversation at home.'

'I don't,' I said at once.

Then she said to Maddy. 'I'll help you pack.' She turned to my parents, 'I'm very sorry about this little misunderstanding.'

'No, it was completely our fault,' replied Mum, looking directly at Dad as she said this.

So you see what happened there, don't you? All four parents joined forces to gang up on Maddy and me. And that's not right, is it? They should at least have considered what we had to say. No wonder Maddy and I were seething.

And she couldn't have got up any more slowly

either. She then said to my dad, 'I really hope the lamb cutlets aren't ruined,' which I thought was extremely thoughtful of her.

Digby called after her. 'I'm sure in time you will embrace this wonderful new opportunity, Maddy.'

I gave that poseur my death glare before following Maddy upstairs. She and I grimly watched her mum pack up Maddy's stuff so quickly she might have been in a race.

Maddy left my house faster than the speed of light.

8.30 p.m.
Maddy's just had a long and a totally pointless conversation with her parents about America. They kept saying to her, 'You must trust us. We know what is best for you.'

But they so don't.

Then she said how proud she was of me tonight – especially that little speech I gave. She hasn't a clue why they all started laughing like loonies after I'd finished either.

It just proves what I've long suspected – all parents are completely bonkers.

8.35 p.m.
Digby is still infecting our house like a bad smell.

When I finally went downstairs I heard him saying to Elliot. 'So you gave up, what is surely your most precious possession – your very own bedroom – just so you could borrow your brother's iPhone.'

And Elliot was replying in what he totally, mistakenly thinks is his adorable voice. 'Yes, that's right, sir. (Sir!) Louis spent hours and hours saying he was going to try and be a better brother to me and talked me into' (his voice wobbled here) 'letting his girlfriend take over my room. All I would get in return was being allowed to borrow his iPhone. Well I should still be allowed to borrow it, shouldn't I? He can't be allowed to go back on our deal now.'

'You treacherous little rattlesnake!' I yelled at him. 'You're not going anywhere near my iPhone ever again. That arrangement is abolished, terminated forever. And get all your moronic stuff out of my bedroom now.'

'No I won't,' he shouted defiantly.

'You will!' I shouted back.

Elliot tried to shout, 'Louis is a massive poo poo!' but it was hard for him to say very much with both my hands clamped over his mouth.

'All right boys, stop this now,' cried Dad in such a sharp tone of voice I let Elliot go at once. 'You have both behaved very badly, not least in deceiving me. But I'm not angry – just very, very disappointed.'

Yeah, Dad was playing that musty old favourite – 'I'm very disappointed', absolutely guaranteed to guilt-trip your kids. Only not this time as I'm the wronged person here, not him, aren't I?

9.00 p.m.
At least my bedroom is an Elliot-free zone again. That's the only good news. But I tried to cheer Maddy up by texting that tonight was only a tiny setback. But neither of us really believes that.

Then I texted her a joke.

Why was Cinderella thrown off the football team?
Because she ran away from the ball.

Maddy thought that was really clever.
So next I sent off a dead silly joke.

Why don't elephants like to go swimming?
Because it's hard to keep their trunks up.

She said that one made her laugh even more.
Sometimes there's nothing better in the whole world than a really silly joke.

Chapter Thirteen

Parents Acting Highly Suspiciously

Wednesday January 15th

Came home to hear Dad gushing away to someone on the phone. 'Thanks for taking it so well. That's very, very good of you. We do appreciate it. Bye.' If he'd curtseyed at the end I wouldn't have been very surprised. He spotted me and said, 'Maddy's dad is able to see the funny side of yesterday now.'

'So that's who you were creeping around,' I said. 'Can't think why.'

'What!' exclaimed Dad.'Come on, Louis, your

behaviour was outrageous yesterday.'

'What did I do?'

'Well for a start you lied to me – and encouraged your brother to lie to me as well.'

'Elliot didn't need any encouraging – and lie is a very strong word ...'

'Then you put your mum and me in a highly embarrassing situation. And as for Maddy's poor parents, they didn't know what was going on ...'

'All I wanted was for my home to be Maddy's too. That's not too much to ask, is it?'

Dad didn't answer me at first. Couldn't, I thought. So I started checking my messages. Then he snapped suddenly. 'If you'd stop messing about on that wretched phone for five whole seconds, then maybe we could discuss this properly.'

I looked up.

'It's infuriating,' Dad moaned on. 'You never put that thing down. So you're not really listening to anything I say.'

'All right, Dad,' I said. 'You have my full and undivided attention. Now will you answer a question?'

'Of course.'

'Can Maddy move in here?'

'You know that's absolutely impossible,'

spluttered Dad.

'No, I don't.'

'Well, it is,' said Dad.

'Then we've got nothing else to say. But I'm glad you and Maddy's dad had a good old laugh about completely ruining two young lives.'

Yeah, I meant that to sting – and I think it did.

Then I carried on checking my messages.

Thursday 16th January

5.00 p.m.

Elliot is in big trouble at school. His form teacher has just been talking to Dad. Apparently he's got very poor concentration (Elliot that is, not my dad), is very easily distracted and isn't stretching himself either. So now Mum and Dad are giving Elliot a right telling off. It cheered me up massively.

5.45 p.m.

Edgar has called round to inform me that he is organising a protest on Saturday morning about Maddy being evacuated to America.

'I shall be reading out a poem I have written about this at the end of Maddy's road,' he announced.

'That should clear the area.'

'It has nine verses.'

'I thought it might,' I murmured, but added graciously, 'well, good luck.'

'I wondered if you'd care to join me?'

I stared at him. 'You don't do jokes, do you?'

'I'll make us both placards. So you can hold one too. I also thought we could stop all the traffic.'

Suddenly he had my interest. It was a completely crazy scheme. But at least I'd be doing something to help Maddy. And I was sure it would amuse her.

'Okay, why not,' I said.

'Now I shall get to work on our placards – but not a word to Maddy. I want this to be a wonderful surprise for her.'

7.00 p.m.

In my bedroom, and deep into a computer game when I just happened to glance up. And that's when I saw it. A shadowy figure in the doorway. But only for a second. Then it was gone.

It gave me quite a shock.

Is my house being haunted by an extremely shy ghost?

A few minutes later I saw the figure loom up in the doorway again. Only this time it lingered

105

long enough for me to recognise it.

'Hi, Dad. Are you lost?'

'Sorry to disturb you,' he said.

'No, feel free to lurk in my doorway anytime. As a matter of interest, what are you doing exactly?'

'Oh ... just watching you. Been here quite a while actually,' replied Dad. 'But nothing for you to worry about,' he added, before promptly disappearing again.

Mysterious or what?

7.40 p.m.

And now it's Mum's turn to haunt my bedroom. I was sending Maddy a funny picture when I spied her, just by the door.

'Not much on telly tonight, Mum?' I said.

'Don't worry, Louis, you're not in trouble,' she said.

'That's a first,' I said.

And with that she left as speedily as Dad.

Even more mysterious.

8.03 p.m.

I've solved the mystery. When I found out that Mum and Dad had been observing Elliot too, I sussed out what was going on.

Homework.

Most of the time my parents leave me to get on with it – or not get on with it, if you want to be boringly accurate. But occasionally they go through a truly tragic phase, when they decide to check how much work I'm actually doing. This is no fun at all for me – or them. The smallest event can trigger off this phase too.

'You caused this,' I hissed at Elliot, 'with your teacher ringing up tonight.'

'I didn't ask her to,' he wailed. 'And anyway, I can't help it if I'm nearly as thick as you.'

Friday 17th January

5.20 p.m.
Yesterday was bad enough, but you won't believe what's happened now. Digby has not only been polluting my house again – but my bedroom too.

I'd only just got back too, when Dad brought him in.

Digby smirked at me. 'You don't mind if we venture into your nest?'

My nest! And I've been dragged away from my iPhone after suffering the misery of school all day, to converse with this boring old maggot.

'So how are you?' asked Digby.

Now it's bad enough when your parents ask you moronic questions like that. But I suppose they're entitled to bore you rigid. Not Smirk-face though. So I mumbled something even I couldn't hear and hoped he'd take the hint. Instead he asked, 'How about if we have a little chat?'

'And how about if you get rid of all the hairs up your nose? It's like a forest up there.'

Okay I never actually said this. But I thought it. Very loudly. While Dad answered for me. (And don't you hate it when parents do that.) 'Louis would love to have a chat with you.'

I gave Dad my worst look, while Digby pranced over to me on his tip-toes (he always walks like that!) and flung down something on to the floor. It was a beanbag. The next thing I knew Digby was sitting cross-legged on it and grinning up at me like an elderly toddler.

'I do this to break down the barriers between us. Now it could be just one of your friends chewing the fat with you,' he said.

Of course it could. My friends always bring a beanbag with them and then sprawl out on it, as if they're about to start performing yoga.

'Sometimes, Louis, I try to imagine what it's like to be thirteen, because I like to put myself in other people's shoes, as that means I can really understand and help them.'

But I didn't want Digby understanding me, EVER. I looked across at Dad. But he was nodding away all enthusiastically as if Gandalf himself was crouched on that beanbag. 'So I've been thinking about being thirteen, and all those challenges you face. Now, tell me, Louis, when we came in you were on your iPhone. Were you texting a friend?'

'No, I was playing a game.'

'And how long will it last?' asked Digby.

I shrugged. Why was he so interested?

'Might it go on for hours?' he asked.

'It might.'

'And you won't get bored?'

Talk about mad questions. 'No.'

'It must demand a huge commitment,' he said.

'I suppose.'

'And after the game is over, Louis, does real life seem extremely dull and colourless?'

For a moment I was almost impressed.

'Yeah, it often does,' I said.

Digby let out a sigh which seemed to fill the whole room. And Dad released a copycat sigh too. I didn't know what they were so depressed about. And then quite suddenly I did.

So I said mega-hastily, 'But I still find time to do my homework. In fact, playing games on my computer sharpens my brain so I get higher marks than I would have done before.'

Digby sprang to his feet. 'This has been most

interesting.'

I was glad one of us had enjoyed themselves.

'But before I go, I'm going to tell you something which will really, really surprise you.' Here it comes I thought. He's going to tell me how when he was a little weasel, he did a trillion hours of homework and that put hairs up his nose, and made him the most annoying person on planet Earth.

But instead he announced, 'I am not carrying a mobile phone. You can search me if you like.'

'No, you're all right,' I said.

'I haven't even forgotten it. I never, ever carry one.' He stopped here to allow me to explode in amazement. And I suppose I sort of did. 'I know how important it is to you, Louis, but here's something else to stun you. I don't miss it. Do you know why?'

'Amaze me.'

'Because I am far too busy living in the moment. And meeting people. Real people. That's worth thinking about isn't it?'

'I bet I'll never stop,' I said.

Then Digby left to loud, appreciative murmurs of thanks from Dad.

And what was the point of that conversation? Not a clue.

Saturday January 18th

Edgar was waiting for me at the end of Maddy's road. He was wearing a suit and tie and his shoes gleamed with polish.

'Off for a job interview after this are you?' I asked. Then I saw he was holding a flask.

'You've brought a flask!' I exclaimed. Edgar really was the oldest thirteen–year-old I'd ever met.

'Don't worry,' he said, 'I have one for you too.' He nodded at the brown bag beside him. 'I have also packed scarves, as the weather forecast is not at all encouraging for this evening.'

'This evening?' I echoed.

'Well, I'm anticipating we shall be here all day and quite a lot of the night too. Is that convenient for you?'

'Why not?' I murmured.

'I also have an umbrella, and some sandwiches.'

'You've thought of everything,' I said.

'I really think I have,' said Edgar. Then he picked up two placards. One said 'SAVE MADDY', the other 'RESCUE MADDY FROM THE TRULY OPPRESSIVE BEHAVIOUR OF HER PARENTS'.

'I thought you'd prefer to hold the simple one,' said Edgar.

'How thoughtful. Come on, let's get this traffic stopped.'

We positioned ourselves at the entrance to Maddy's road.

'I am just going to text Maddy to look out of her window,' said Edgar.

The first car pulled up. It was a woman with her son. 'What's going on?' she called out of her window.

'We're extremely sorry to inconvenience you,' said Edgar, 'but we are protesting about a miscarriage of justice – to Maddy, who I imagine you know.'

'Oh yes, we know Maddy, don't we?' said the woman to her son. He didn't answer. He was too busy filming us on his phone.

'But what's happened to her?' asked the woman.

'My poem will explain everything,' said Edgar, handing her a copy from a huge pile. He must have printed hundreds.

'It's only nine verses,' I murmured.

'I shall now read it out aloud,' said Edgar.

'As I read, feel free to honk your horn to show solidarity. And afterwards we sincerely hope you will be the first to sign our online petition.'

The woman could only goggle at us open-mouthed as Edgar began reading.

He'd reached the third verse when another car noisily pulled up. The driver – a man with the reddest face I'd ever seen – blasted over to us and bellowed. 'This is not the place for games, children. Move out of the way now!'

'I'm not a child!' Edgar was furious.

'And he never has been, either,' I added.

'But we need you to listen to my poem,' said Edgar.

'The time will just fly by,' I said.

Now say what you like about Edgar – he has got a certain mad courage. I mean, I'm not sure I would have dared to hand a copy of my poem to this red-faced guy who by now was breathing fire. Let alone carry on reciting it.

But Edgar was soon interrupted again. Maddy was tearing over to us. 'This is so brilliant of you both,' she cried.

'Well, it was mostly Edgar,' I said.

He nodded in agreement.

'But you must both stop now,' Maddy said very firmly. This wasn't at all the reaction Edgar – or I actually – had been expecting. But she was so definite, we let the two cars go past – the red-faced man hurling Edgar's poem out of the car as he sped off.

'Litter lout!' I called after him.

Then Maddy motioned for us to follow her. But

why on earth did she want us to finish protesting when we'd hardly started? I helped Edgar pack away, the two placards, now drooping dejectedly, under his arm.

Maddy waited for us outside her house, which now, I noticed with a shudder, had a TO LET sign planted beside it.

'I'd barely begun my poem about your plight,' Edgar said, quivering with indignation.

'I know,' said Maddy. 'It's fantastic you've gone to so much trouble. But honestly, there's no point. Do you know what my parents are doing at this very moment?'

'No,' I said, 'but I shock easily.'

'They're in there with some geezer from the American company who have headhunted Dad – and they're all just so excited and happy. I can't stand it. And later today Mum and Dad have arranged for this British family in America, including their daughter, who they say I will absolutely love,' Maddy made a face, 'to talk to us on Skype and tell us how wonderful their lives are now and—'

'So you're just throwing in the towel?' interrupted Edgar.

'I'm not going to waste my last precious weeks here trying to change their minds, when I know it's completely impossible. But I haven't thrown

in the towel. In fact, I've made my own protest.'
A small smile flashed across her face.

'What have you done?' I demanded at once.

'Come inside for a moment,' Maddy whispered,
'but be really quiet as my parents don't suspect
it's got anything to do with me.'

Highly intrigued, Edgar and I deposited our
placards and Edgar's bulging bag outside by the
door. Inside we heard the rumble of a deeply
boring conversation from the kitchen. Maddy
beckoned us into the living room.

'Normally they'd have brought him in here,'
she hissed, 'but today they didn't dare.'

The room looked perfectly normal until a
huge gust of whiffiness blasted right into my
face. 'Eeer,' I began.

Maddy giggled. 'What do you think it is?'

'Well,' I said, 'it reminds me of when I was
on this train and I thought the man in the seat
behind me was doing the smelliest farts ever. It
was truly disgusting. But it turned out he was
stuffing his face with Scotch eggs. But actually
I'd say this stink is even worse.'

Maddy's face was one big smile now. 'And it's
all thanks to me.'

'What on earth have you done?' demanded
Edgar.

'I've hidden a dead fish down the back of the

sofa,' she replied proudly.

Edgar reeled. I was doing a spot of reeling too.

'You both looked so stunned,' she said. 'You thought I was too sensible and boring to ever do this, didn't you?'

'No,' I began. 'Only it isn't the sort of thing you normally do. But way to go, Maddy, and respect – that stink really is terrible.'

'Every day it'll get worse too,' she said eagerly. 'My parents keep opening the windows and immediately I close them again and switch up the heating. They can't work out what's causing it either and—'

Maddy was interrupted by an extremely odd noise.

It sounded like a seal with a very bad throat.

In fact, it was Edgar. And he was laughing.

Sunday January 19th

11.00 a.m.

Dead suspicious.

Mum has just announced she wants to give Elliot and me 'a treat'. So she is taking us both out for a meal. Nothing wrong with that, you might say. Only there is.

I mean, Elliot's form teacher has just given him a truly rubbish report while my parents are still going on about the deeply awkward situation I put them in with Maddy and her parents. Of course, I see it totally differently (and I'm right).

But my point is, why, after all that hassle, should Mum suddenly want to give Elliot and me a treat?

1.20 p.m.
Mum is being far too nice, saying stuff like, 'Today you can eat whatever you want. And I promise not to say a word about any of your choices,' and then laughing merrily.

Well, of course I wasn't going to turn down any excuse to fill my face. But afterwards I started wondering what the catch could be.

'Where's Dad again?' I asked her.

'At home,' she replied, a little too casually.

'But why didn't he come with us?' I asked.

'Well, actually he's preparing a surprise for you both.'

'Awesome!' cried Elliot.

I stared at him contemptuously. He knows so little about the ways of parents.

'What sort of surprise?' I queried, warily.

'If I told you that,' said Mum smiling away, 'it wouldn't be a surprise, would it?'

'Well just tell me this,' I persisted. 'Will we

like it?'

Mum hesitated for a fraction of a second before gushing, 'Oh, I'm sure you will.'

Rough translation – we are going to completely hate it.

1.45 p.m.

While Mum is paying the bill I hiss at Elliot, 'You know what the surprise is, don't you?'

'No, what?'

'A tutor. And it's your fault. You are doing so badly at school, they've panicked. And I bet they drag me into it as well. You want to know something else? That tutor is waiting at home for us now.'

Elliot's eyes were like saucers. 'Not on a Sunday afternoon.'

'Oh yeah, this meal is merely to soften us up. Dad is with him now. And this tutor will be someone exactly like Digby. In fact it might even be—'

That's when Elliot let out a yelp of total horror.

Chapter Fourteen

The Worst Idea Ever

Sunday January 19th

4.25 p.m.

All the way home I scared myself with the thought that Digby was my new tutor. I couldn't think of anything more terrible.

BUT NOW I CAN.

At home Dad was as bright as a button. 'Let me introduce you ...' he began. Here it comes, I thought. The moment when Digby springs out at us, laughing maniacally.

'To the treats cupboard,' Dad went on.

And he led us to the cupboard in the kitchen which used to be where deeply boring cleaning stuff hung out, and is now where deeply boring games like Monopoly, Cluedo and Scrabble hang out.

'Well, I'm sure you'll both have hours of fun in here,' I said.

'Oh, we all will,' said Mum.

Of course, I had much, much better things to do, but I pretended to be interested. I'm good like that. And I was about to heave a truly massive sigh of relief that the surprise was not what I'd feared, when Dad announced it was time for a family meeting.

These are a total yawn fest, where we all gather round a table and Mum and Dad deliver a big lecture.

But today Mum and Dad seemed so genial.

'Wonderful to actually see your faces,' grinned Dad.

'It certainly is,' said Mum.

'Because normally they're glued to a screen,' said Dad. 'And you don't look up for hours and hours.'

'Bit of an exaggeration,' I murmured.

'No, Louis, it's not. We've been watching you,' Mum went on.

So that's why they were skulking about by my bedroom door recently.

'But we're not blaming you two,' said Dad.

'It's our fault.'

That's when I became very uneasy. When parents apologise to you – well, just watch out.

'You've seen us constantly on our phones and laptops,' said Mum, 'so it's no wonder you've started copying us.'

'Mum, I really haven't,' I assured her.

'We're spending less time together as a family than ever before,' proclaimed Dad. 'Why? Because we're all too busy peering at screens.'

'Don't take it personally,' I said, kindly. 'That's just how people live now, because the internet is way more interesting than us.'

'I don't agree,' blurted Dad so loudly even Mum stared at him. In a quieter voice he continued. 'I believe we're losing something very precious. Like all the memories we four can share and remember forever. So that's why from eight o'clock tonight—'

'Curfew time,' cut in Mum.

'Exactly,' said Dad.

Elliot and I gaped at them. What were they gabbling on about now?

'From eight o'clock tonight,' announced Mum, 'we're having a digital detox, I think it's called. No one will use any computers, laptops, phones, tablets ...'

'You've got to be joking!' I cried.

'We're not,' said Dad. 'All electronic media will be banned in this house, for one week. To start with.'

'To start with!' I jumped up.

'Where are you going?' asked Dad.

'To ring Childline,' I replied. 'No child should be made to live without an iPhone.'

'But we're going to have such an excellent time,' said Mum.

'Doing what?' asked Elliot.

'Well, for a start, we're not only going to be playing board games at Christmas,' grinned Dad. 'We can play them whenever we want. Every night, if we like.'

'Just kill me now,' I murmured.

'But we can do other things too,' said Mum brightly. 'Like going for long walks.'

'It'll be freezing,' I said.

'And I hate walking,' said Elliot.

'Or we can go to the park,' said Dad.

'Play on the swings in January, you mean?' I interrupted. 'Everyone will think we're insane.' Then I thought of something else. 'And how will we contact anyone?'

'You'll just have to do what your mum and I did way back in the 1970s and 1980s,' grinned Dad. 'Use the trusty old landline.'

'But none of our friends know our number,' I

said. '*I* don't even know our number.'

'You've got until eight o'clock to spread the deeply tragic news that your friends can only speak to you on an ordinary phone,' said Mum. 'Don't worry, you'll soon get used to it.'

'But I don't want to,' I said. 'It's just so weird.'

'We'll be the freaky kids,' wailed Elliot. Then he added, 'And what about doing our homework?'

Mum replied. 'We'll talk to your teachers, tell them what we're doing. And if the use of a computer is absolutely vital for a piece of work, you can switch it on in the living room, with your Dad or me supervising. But we will also have on the table an encyclopaedia, a dictionary and a thesaurus ...'

'Mum, why bother with all that? You can find out anything on Google in seconds,' I said.

'This will be much more fun though,' she said.

I stared at her. 'Really, Mum, really?'

'I'm taking a few days off work,' she said, 'so I will be here to help. And we do realise this requires more effort from both of you, but it really will be worth it.'

'You can guarantee that, can you?' I asked.

'I think we're all going to benefit from this experiment – your dad and me too,' said Mum. 'And we can't wait to get started.'

'And really start connecting with each other

again,' said Dad.

5.10 p.m.
Rang Maddy. 'I just wanted to let you know I shall be travelling back to the 1970s at eight o'clock tonight.'

Then I explained.

'But they can't just uninvent things!' she cried.

'Oh, my parents can! They say we're going to have marvellous fun playing moth-eaten old board games and scampering about in the park.'

Then I gave her my landline number.

'I don't know who's worse – your parents or mine,' she muttered.

'Right now, I'd say it was a draw,' I replied, and then I added, 'How's the stink?'

'So smelly you wouldn't believe. Now my parents think it must be the drains.'

'Even on a dark day like today,' I said, 'there's always something to cheer you up.'

6.35 p.m.
I've finally managed to get Mum on her own. 'Mum!' I burst out. 'How is this happening? And was Dad conscious when he decided this?'

'It was a joint decision, actually,' said Mum. 'And I know we're all going to miss stuff at first.

But who says we still can't have a great time?'

'Er, me.'

7.15 p.m.

I'm so desperate, I have joined forces with Elliot to hatch a last minute plan. Told Elliot exactly what to say. It *has* to work.

7.25 p.m.

Listened outside the door as Elliot moved solemnly into the living room. 'Very sorry to disturb you,' he said to my parents (good start).

'Don't be silly,' said Dad.

Elliot went on in this high, breathy voice, 'I'll follow you into this experiment tonight.'

'Thank you, Elliot,' said Mum. 'We appreciate that.'

Elliot's voice rose here, just as I'd told him. 'But don't take the twenty-first century away from Louis. All right, make him play Scrabble and Monopoly if you must, but spare him his iPhone. For if you take that away you'll be tearing out his heart.'

'What a moving speech,' muttered Dad.

'Yes,' agreed Elliot.

'And I expect Louis will be making a similar speech about you soon, won't he?' went on Dad.

'That's right,' agreed Elliot again. 'I mean ...

'err, no he won't, he'll … he'll …' He struggled to recover, but it was too late. The total clown.

Then Mum called, 'Nice try, Louis. You are listening outside, aren't you?'

I put my head round the door. 'Do you know, I just happened to be passing and heard my name mentioned. And then I was just so moved by what Elliot said …'

'Yes, you coached him well,' said Mum.

'But it won't work this time,' said Dad firmly.

7.50 p.m.
Even more desperate now (and I was completely desperate before). That's why I've just told my parents, 'I'll do a deal with you. I'll empty the dishwasher every night and make my bed every day and never leave my socks lying about. I'd even feed the cat, if we had a cat, only we don't have one. But I'll buy us a cat and feed it and do anything else you want on one condition: you let me have my iPhone for one weeny hour a night. Two at the weekends.'

They had to say 'Yes' to that, I thought. I was offering them so much. Bargain of the year, in fact. Neither Mum nor Dad spoke at first, merely rolled their eyes at each other.

'Isn't this fascinating?' said Mum at last.

'It really is,' agreed Dad, 'that Louis would go

to such lengths. It shows what a hold all this new technology—'

'I am still in the room you know,' I interrupted.

'I'm going to make a prediction, Louis,' said Dad.

'I'd rather you let me use my iPhone,' I interrupted.

'A week from now you'll wonder what all this fuss was about, because you'll be having so much fun without all these modern trappings,' beamed Dad.

And you know what, they both really believe that. My mum and dad have totally lost the plot this time, haven't they?

8.15 p.m.

'Let's do this, buddies!' said Dad as he collected away Elliot's tablet and my iPhone and iPad in a box.

'Do I get a receipt?' I asked.

Then the landline rang, making us all jump. It was Maddy.

'Welcome to the 1970s,' she said.

Chapter Fifteen

Living in the 1970s

Monday January 20th

7.20 a.m.
Dad has just asked me how I slept.

'Very badly,' I replied. 'I had this total nightmare that I couldn't use my iPhone any more. Thank goodness it was all a dream.'

He didn't show the slightest flicker of conscience though.

After he left I stared around my deadly silent bedroom, as the full horror of my situation began to hit me. All the exciting, funny stuff is still happening – BUT WITHOUT ME. I'm not part of it any more. In fact, I am totally cut off from all civilisation.

8.05 a.m.

That ancient form of telephonic communication known as the landline rang again. And this time it made Dad jump so much he dropped two eggs. 'We'll soon get used to it,' he said.

It was Maddy again.

'After school,' she said, 'come to my house. I've had an idea.'

'Tell me more.'

'That Vintage Clothes shop next to my school is having a big sale.'

'Well ...'

'Well, I've Googled up the 1970s,' she said.

'Google? What is the meaning of that strange, alien word?'

'And I'm sure,' she continued, 'some of the clothes are gross enough to have come from the 1970s. So, I thought, if your parents are making you time-travel, you might as well look the part. Do you dig my idea?'

'Do I what?'

'I've looked up some 1970s slang too. And dig means like.'

'In that case,' I said, 'I really dig what you're saying.'

'So I'll catch you on the flipside,' said Maddy.

'In the 1970s that means see you later.'

4.05 p.m.

I am now wearing a purple shirt, with the widest collar you have ever seen, the yellowest yellow trousers in the world (even yellower than Digby's) and a truly hideous cowboy hat. This is all topped off with a glittery scarf, which no human could ever have put on voluntarily.

I got changed at Maddy's, bunging all my school uniform into an old bag. Her mum was in the garden with two guys from a company specialising in drains. But she came in just as Maddy and I shot down the stairs.

'Louis!' Maddy's mum said my name in a kind of shocked squeak.

'Hi there,' I said. 'You're looking well.'

'But what ...' she stuttered. 'What on earth are you wearing?'

'Maddy's bought it all for me. Hasn't she got excellent taste?'

Before she could reply, Maddy and I dashed outside and then laughed and laughed.

4.30 p.m.

Arrived home to find Mum and Elliot in the living room in front of a roaring fire. He was fiddling about with a Rubik's cube and Mum was doing a crossword. 'Hey rock chick, how's it grooving?' I said.

At first Mum could only gape at me, while the Rubik's cube flew out of Elliot's hand as he doubled over with laughter. Finally Mum managed to gasp, 'Louis, why on earth are you dressed like that?'

'I wanted to look the part, doll-face, and lay the cool vibe on you,' I said, throwing in some of the 70s slang Maddy had taught me. 'Does it bring back lots of happy memories for you?'

'No, it doesn't.' Then a look of horror crossed her face. 'You didn't walk down the road like that?'

'Of course I did – and quite a few neighbours saw me. One even waved.'

You could almost hear Mum's teeth grinding together. Then she asked. 'But where's your school uniform? Not squashed up in that little bag?'

'That's right, Mum.'

Elliot began giggling madly again as if he'd had a huge dose of laughing gas.

'Take if off now,' she snapped.

'But, Mum, these threads are far out!' Then Dad came in and did a massive double-take.

'Hey, Daddy Cool,' I said. 'How's it hanging? You can borrow my new clothes if you like.'

Elliot was rolling about on the carpet now, he was finding it so hysterically funny.

Dad was just stunned. 'For a second there I didn't even recognise you ...' he began.

'Hey, Dad, you're the man!' I yelled. 'And, Mum, just so you don't feel left out, you're the man too.'

'Enough,' cried Mum. 'Go upstairs and get changed now. And Elliot, get up off the carpet.'

Mum sounded so annoyed I danced all the way up the stairs.

5.00 p.m.

In my bedroom and still in some of my 1970s gear when I heard Dad pounding up the stairs. I quickly switched off all the lights. And when he poked his head round the door I called out, 'Dad, have you got any candles?'

'Yeah, they're ... but what's happened?'

'All my lights have gone out,' I spluttered.

'What can have caused that?' he sounded so alarmed I started to shake as I said, 'must be a power cut. Apparently they were very big in the 1970s.'

'Very funny,' said Dad switching on the lights. 'You had me going there.' He smiled reminiscently. 'The lights always seemed to go out just as we were about to have a meal.'

'The good old days,' I muttered.

Dad plonked himself down on my bed. 'You haven't got changed yet.'

'No, Dad, because this is really helping me dig the 1970s groove. Do you think I could wear this to school tomorrow?'

'All right, Louis,' said Dad. 'We know what we're doing is a big thing to ask of you. And you'll probably get a few withdrawal symptoms over the next few days and weeks ...'

'The next few *weeks* ...' I interrupted, my voice rising. 'Exactly how long is this going on for?'

'Ah,' said Dad.

I've never heard a more sinister 'Ah' in my life.

6.05 p.m.

I burst into Elliot's room. 'What are you doing?'

He stared guiltily. 'My homework.'

'But if you begin acting like a good boy then they'll think this insane experiment is working.'

Elliot immediately flung his pen down.

'And Dad's just told me,' I lowered my voice, 'we could be living in the house time forgot for weeks. We've got to put a stop to it.'

'How?' asked Elliot.

'Well, for a start, we must keep reminding Dad and Mum – especially Mum – of everything they're missing. And then we've got to look miserable and bored all the time. Give me a quick sample of your moody face.'

Elliot demonstrated.

'You look constipated. But it'll do – and yawn a lot.'

'I'm very good at yawning,' said Elliot.

7.05 p.m.

Mum and Dad must have noticed how fed up and gloomy Elliot and I looked during the family meal, because afterwards, in the eerily silent living room, Dad said, 'I'd like to remind a couple of members of our team that this is not a punishment.'

'It only feels like one,' I muttered.

'Look on this,' said Dad, 'as a journey we're all going on together.'

'Why don't you two go on ahead,' I said, 'and tell us about it later.'

7.15 p.m.

Time moves very slowly in the 1970s.

I KNOW.

Mum and Dad have scattered board games, crossword books and puzzles everywhere.

'Feel free to look at whatever interests you,' said Mum, sounding like a very eager shop assistant. 'We've bought lots of new things too.'

'Be spontaneous,' added Dad. So I very spontaneously switched on the television.

Mum looked up from her colouring book ('Amazingly therapeutic,' she kept saying) and let out a very shocked, 'Oh!'

'Television was around in the 1970s, wasn't it?' I asked.

'Of course it was,' replied Mum, a bit snappily. 'And if there's a programme we'd want to watch as a family – that's great. So can you find something you think we'd all enjoy, Louis?'

'I didn't realise I had to take an exam now before I could watch anything,' I said, and switched the television off again.

7.41 p.m.

Mum has just found me crouched in the cupboard where we keep all the coats and shoes. 'Louis, what on earth are you doing in here?' she demanded.

'It's dead exciting,' I said.

'What are you talking about?'

'Well, Dad hasn't changed into his slippers yet. So I've got that to look forward to. And later, you and Dad might go for a walk and come and get the coats. So there's my whole evening's entertainment sorted out.'

135

She gave a very faint smile. 'You haven't given tonight a chance.'

Now, I like to spread good cheer, but there are moments when you have to be honest. And this was one of them. 'Mum, I'm not going to lie. I've never been more bored in my life.'

'Excellent!' cried Mum to my total astonishment. Then she called out to Dad, 'Louis says he's bored!'

He looked chuffed to bits too as he came over. 'Out of boredom, Louis, comes real creativity. You see up to now you've been relying on gadgets to distract you. And you're missing them. We've been told to expect this response.'

I pounced on this. 'Who told you to expect this response?' Then I answered my own question. 'But of course, Digby's put you up to this, hasn't he.'

'No ...' began Dad.

'Yes he has!' I cried, knocking down several pairs of shoes in my excitement. 'He hasn't got a mobile phone, and spends his time bothering strangers instead. And now he's infected you with his crackpot theories.'

'No, Digby has just encouraged us to think outside the box,' began Dad. He was interrupted by Elliot thundering down the stairs. Insanely, I thought he might be coming to back me up.

Instead he shouted, 'Just to tell you, I've just had an awesome idea for a story and I can't wait to write it!'

Mum and Dad beamed with pride. 'See what I mean, Louis,' Dad said triumphantly. 'Give this a chance and who knows what you might do.'

Right now there was something I wanted to do all right. Throttle Elliot.

8.55 p.m.

On the coldest night of the century my parents INSISTED we all go out, as a family, for a walk. 'It will do us so much good,' they kept saying.

And on the way to the park they kept pointing out stuff like, 'Look, there's a tree. And, see, over there are some berries,' just as if we were on safari or something.

Of course, the park was completely deserted, except for a couple of people walking their dogs.

'Will you look at them,' whispered Dad contemptuously, 'staring down at their phones and missing everything.'

Actually, on a bleak, miserable night like this, when there was absolutely nothing to see, it seemed completely sensible to be looking down at your phone. And anyway, both of the dog walkers did glance up at us enthusing over a twig or something. And I know exactly what they were thinking.

In fact, we may as well have had 'We're a family of loons' tattooed across our heads.

But my treacherous little brother was skipping about, still burbling on about the amazing story he'd written.

Then Dad started droning on about his precious tree house and how he was outside all the time when he was my age.

'So was I!' cried Mum, getting all excited. 'Picking blackberries, looking for frogspawn, having picnics, finding conkers – whatever happened to all those simple pleasures?'

'Everyone's upgraded, Mum,' I replied.

9.05 p.m.
I've only had one day living like I'm in some weird sect. So the agony has hardly begun. And already I don't know how much more I can take.

Perhaps I should start acting mad. Sit downstairs with my pants on my head while eating a packet of custard powder.

But you know what, I don't think my parents would be that bothered. They're so convinced what they're doing is right. Digby has totally brainwashed them. So now they're not my parents any more. They're Digby clones.

9.08 p.m.

Is it too late to ask to be adopted? I'll take anyone with a good broadband connection.

Tuesday January 21st

8.05 a.m.

Strutted down to breakfast in my full 1970s kit.

'You don't mind if I wear this to school, do you?' I ask – waiting for them to come over all parenty.

Instead Dad actually grins. 'That get-up does bring back so many memories.'

'It certainly does,' agrees Mum. 'So the next time you have an out of uniform day at school you can definitely wear it.'

'In fact, we'll insist on it,' laughs Dad.

They then started yattering on about the awful clothes they used to wear.

But I haven't done this for them to enjoy themselves. No, this is a protest. Only they haven't even noticed.

Marvellous.

4.35 p.m.

Arrived home to find Elliot in a lather of excitement.

'Dad's still away at one of his courses,' he

burst out, 'and Mum's had to go whooshing off, as there's a huge crisis at her work. And no one knew how to contact her.'

'Because of her living in another century, probably.'

'So,' said Elliot looking at me all expectantly.

'So,' I repeated.

'We can go and look for our phones and tablets,' he said.

I was extremely ashamed I hadn't thought of that myself. 'But aren't you enjoying yourself in ye olden days?' I said.

'Sort of,' he admitted, 'but I miss my tablet.'

And I so missed my iPhone. So we charged upstairs. The first place we looked was Mum and Dad's bedroom – where they store the Christmas presents. And with a startling lack of originality, that was where they'd hidden all the phones and stuff too.

Elliot snatched up his tablet and let out a low, gulping sound. Powerful feelings permeated me too, as I examined my iPhone. Happily it seemed to be in perfect health.

And I started connecting with the world again. I felt as if I'd been unplugged for decades not two days.

I quickly checked my messages.

We were so totally absorbed neither of us

heard the front door open or a familiar voice call out. We didn't even hear two pair of footsteps pound up the stairs.

Then the bedroom door sprang open.

Chapter Sixteen

Full of Snow

4.35 p.m.

Dad gave a pained sigh. 'Boys, I'm so disappointed.' The person with him just smirked in a superior sort of way. Yeah, that's right, it was Digby.

'It was Louis's idea – he made me do it,' bleated Elliot. You can always rely on Little Legs to let you down.

I didn't back down though. 'We were merely,' I said, 'checking our property which has been illegally taken from us.'

'Put your devices down, gentlemen,' said Digby in his quiet, whispery voice.

At once I was fizzing with irritation. He

couldn't tell me what to do. So while Elliot flung his tablet down on to the bed, I still held tightly on to my iPhone.

'Louis,' said Dad warningly.

Finally, I placed my phone on to the bed too, but so gently you wouldn't have been very surprised if I'd started humming it a lullaby. I kept a little smile playing about my lips too because – well, I'm cool like that.

'The important thing,' said Digby, staring at us so gravely you'd have thought we'd robbed fifty banks before breakfast, 'is not to let our mistakes define us. I want you to look on this as a learning moment, gentlemen.' (I can't tell you how much I hated the way he kept calling us that.)

'Now, what do you think you've learnt from your experience?'

'Not to get caught,' I suggested.

Dad gave a loud groan. And Digby said we need to have a proper conversation about this, but first we must do some breathing exercises to relieve all the tension in the room.

I was just wondering how much more of Digby I could stand today when Elliot yelled out, 'Look, it's snowing!'

Outside, snowflakes were indeed madly whirling everywhere. The first snow of the winter is always a genius moment, but today was even more special because Digby's face had become very tense indeed as he asked fearfully, 'You don't think it's settling?'

'Oh it really is,' I said, without even looking. 'In fact, you've got some snow on you already – oh no, it's dandruff.'

'Behave, Louis,' warned Dad.

But Digby was saying, 'I really don't want to get stuck in that.'

'You so don't,' I agreed.

'So,' said Digby 'I shall have to enjoy your hospitality another time.'

'But I thought you wanted to see how our experiment is progressing,' said Dad, 'and give us some tips as to how to …'

'Just continue to replace virtual experiences with real experiences,' interrupted Digby, who was already tumbling down the stairs at an incredible speed.

'You'll be fine, Digby,' I yelled after him. 'Just do lots of deep breathing exercises.'

9.02 p.m.
Mum and Dad have now hidden our phones in another place. But the massive telling off I'd been expecting never happened. All thanks to the snow.

144

Throughout the meal we all looked out at it still pelting down, and as soon as we'd finished we all surged outside. I was shouting jokes like:

What's an ig?
A snow house without a loo.

And:

What do you call a gangsta snowman?
Fros-T

And then Dad started spouting, 'Isn't this better than staring at screens? Now we can live in the moment and ... Ouch.'

That's when I lobbed a snowball at him.

Only a small one. But Dad hurled one right back at me. Caught me in the back of the head too.

And soon it was total war. Even Mum joined in. It was ages before we noticed it had actually stopped snowing.

'That was brilliant,' said Elliot.

For once I could agree with him.

'What would you like to do now?' asked Dad.

I said, 'I'd like to return to my own time and check Snapchat and Instagram, then play a computer game and ...'

'How about a game of Monopoly instead?' interrupted Dad.

'I'd rather stab my eyeballs with a fork,' I muttered.

But Dad was off down memory lane again. 'You know, when I was a boy I don't think I was ever closer to your granddad than when we were playing Monopoly. We'd often play for hours and hours too.'

So out came the battered old Monopoly board with the sellotape down the middle. And Mum brought in a tray of hot chocolate and some fondant fancies – they were even trying to eat themselves back into the past. They were delicious though, I'll admit that.

But Monopoly.

It's fine on Boxing Day afternoon. Well, it's not even fine then, actually. But you've had some good presents and it stops all your relations from talking to you for a bit.

But whose idea of a good time is to play it at the end of January when there are at least a zillion more interesting things I could be doing.

And then, when I've finally escaped to my bedroom, Mum pops up again, this time with a dusty old jigsaw puzzle in her hand and says I might like to start it before I go to sleep.

This madness really has got to stop now.

But how?

11.08 p.m.
Yeah, still awake but I've had a brainwave.
Well, a microwave anyway.
I'm sending Maddy an SOS.
Here it is.

11.10 p.m.
Hi Maddy
IT'S ELEVEN O'CLOCK AT NIGHT AND, YEAH, I'M
WRITING YOU A LETTER.

Apparently in bygone days people did this quite
a lot. Edgar probably still does. What do you bet
he's got his own quill?

But proper communication is me sending you
silly jokes all day, isn't it?

I tell you, Maddy, it's taken me just two days
to realise that without iPhones life is totally
barbaric.

Occasionally (like every five minutes) I've
pointed out to my parents all the things they're
missing. So I said to my mum tonight, 'You could
be settling down now to watch all those funny
cat videos you love. I bet even now they've added
one of a cat in a big hat, dancing and playing the
piano.'

Do you know what she said? 'What's really

147

special is spending time with your family.'

What can you do when your parents are as deluded as that?

And they won't tell me when this crazy experiment will end either. It could go on for weeks (months, even) as they're having a great time revisiting their past – and of course are totally unaware of my miserable existence.

So what do I do, Maddy?

I suppose I could always get a dead fish and stick it down the back of the sofa too. Don't think I haven't been tempted.

Have you got any other suggestions? I'd be insanely grateful if you have. And can you reply in the same antique way as quickly as possible.

Time for a joke.

Why don't elephants use computers?

They're afraid of the mouse.

With kindest regards,

From your boyfriend, Louis X

P.S. What do you call a gorilla with bananas in its ears?

Anything you like. It can't hear you.

Chapter Seventeen

Operation In My Parents' Face

Wednesday January 22nd

8.10 a.m.
Trudged through the nowhere deep enough snow to Maddy's house. She opened the door. 'So this is what it's come to,' I said. 'Me delivering you a letter. We could be back in Victorian times.'

'I think it's kind of cute. Oh,' Maddy added, 'they found the fish last night.'

'Holy ... I'm guessing they didn't have a merry laugh about it.'

'I'm grounded until further notice and they're

very, very shocked,' she giggled.

'What!'

'They are completely convinced it was your idea.'

'I just feel so proud.'

Maddy's mum appeared. 'Hurry up, Maddy,' she said 'or you'll be late for school.' Then, kind of under her breath, 'Good morning, Louis.'

'Hi there – and if you want any more fish, let me know won't you?' Her mum swept away while Maddy's face was one big smile now. 'Answer my letter as soon as you can,' I said. 'And preferably sooner.'

8.15 a.m.

And now I've no way of contacting Maddy for the rest of the day. I'm completely cut off from her. I can't send her a joke or a picture or even a smiley face. Let alone a message.

Actually, I do feel sorry for my parents having to live like this when they were my age. They were truly deprived.

I'd so much rather have grown up in say, the Stone-Age days. Well, school hadn't been invented for a start. And living in a cave would be amazing. And dinosaurs would keep things exciting. But there's not one good thing about my parents' time. How on earth did they stand it?

I suppose the answer is they didn't know any better and were just grateful they weren't being pushed up chimneys any more.

BUT I DO KNOW BETTER.

So I'm being forced to live a totally unnatural life. In fact, I bet most teenagers would have cracked by now.

4.20 p.m.

When I got home a big fat letter from Maddy was waiting on the mat for me.

Dad saw me with it. 'Is that from Maddy, by any chance?'

'I reckon so.'

'You're both entering into the spirit of this, aren't you?

'Oh we really are,' I said.

Before I go any further, I'm going to let you into a secret. I really liked getting a letter, especially as Maddy had decorated it with doodles and a drawing of a four leaf clover, while round the edges in tiny handwriting she'd scribbled gossip from the web.

I shall definitely keep it.

Most importantly, she'd come up with an idea too. It's called, 'Operation In My Parents' Face,' (ace title) and the plan is for me to be with my parents ALL THE TIME.

Wherever they look, there I will be, demanding their attention until they BEG me to go away and to play a computer game.

Maddy thinks I should begin by pestering them with homework questions. Actually, I haven't got any homework tonight – none that I can remember anyway. But fear not, Maddy has very helpfully provided me with masses of (to me) totally unintelligible things to ask for my pretend homework.

5.20 p.m.
Mum and Dad have been racing about trying to help me research my fake homework.

Then Dad asked, 'Why don't we let Louis Google it? We said we'd allow him to use the computer ...'

'I think we should see what the encyclopaedia says first,' replied Mum.

'But won't that take a lot longer?' began Dad.

'It'll be so much more rewarding though,' replied Mum.

On and on they argued. Excellent! In the end Mum won. It is taking them ages though. And they don't know I've got tons more stuff to ask them too.

*   *   *

6.35 p.m.

We're eating very late tonight owing to all the research needed for my homework – and the encyclopaedia being completely out of date.

6.58 p.m.

Now I'm in the kitchen asking Mum lots of questions about cooking and everything else I can think of. Another of Maddy's ideas. She also said I should get into Mum's personal space as much as possible, which means standing right in front of Mum, especially when she's got a hot saucepan in her hand.

7.20 p.m.

I have enthusiastically suggested that we all play a game of football in the park. I'm fairly certain Mum gave a low groan before saying, 'Yes, of course, that would be great fun.'

7.55 p.m.

Another freezing cold night. And we'd just started off when Mum tripped and landed on some dog poo. She valiantly insisted on playing on even when an over-enthusiastic Elliot fouled her several times. Dad also kept getting out of breath, and at one point became so confused he managed to score an own goal.

8.25 p.m.

As soon as we got home, Dad fell asleep in the chair. Of course I woke him up instantly to tell him I urgently needed help researching another project for school (courtesy of Maddy, of course). He and Mum went hobbling off to dig through the boxes of old, dead books in the garage.

9.15 p.m.

Mum and Dad have just staggered into my bedroom looking shattered.

This is it.

The strain of so much of my company has proved too much for them. All they want now is to see as little as possible of me. 'Come and sit down,' I said, as I hate to see the elderly in pain. But it is for their own good as well as mine.

'We'll certainly sleep tonight,' said Mum. She and Dad laughed heartily. 'We just want to say …' began Mum.

I waited tensely.

'We're so pleased to see you taking so much interest in your homework. You can see what we meant now, can't you?'

'Can I?' I asked in a dry whisper.

'Not having so much distraction is really helping you to focus, isn't it?'

'Well …' I began.

'And now we've found this really wonderful encyclopaedia!' cried Mum excitedly. 'I'm going to take a look through it while you're at school tomorrow and then we can study it together in the evening.'

'Oh, I hate to put you to all that bother,' I said.

'It's no bother at all,' she cooed. 'I'm finding out so much too.'

Then Dad joined in, 'And you know something else?'

'What?' I croaked.

'Tonight, the word 'family' just got a bit bigger.'

9.24 p.m.
With normal parents, Maddy's plan would have worked all right. And they'd be begging me to leave them alone now. But with my parents … it's as if Digby has hypnotised them. And I can't seem to un-hypnotise them.

Thursday January 23rd

7.58 a.m.
All through breakfast Mum and Dad kept giving me big smiles. They think I've totally signed up to this trip back to ye olden days now.

4.45 p.m.

I have spent forty-five whole minutes with my mum droning on and on about all the stuff she's found for my project, which is totally made up anyway.

And then, just when you think life can't get any more horrible, Elliot's teacher rings up. Elliot has gained his highest ever mark for the story he wrote on Thursday.

'Thanks to you,' I hissed at him, 'I doubt we'll ever see our phones again now, you total imbecile.'

'You're only jealous,' he squeaked.

6.20 p.m.

Right out of the blue Poppy has rung me.

'I hear you're living in a time slip?' she said.

'Did Maddy tell you?' I asked.

'Yeah. It must be so awful.'

'Not really, I mean mobile phones will be invented in about thirty years. I can wait. By the way, I saw you on *Blue Peter*. And you were so brilliant. I'm not at all surprised you've got Noah and Lily as your fans. And – oh yes, I hate you.'

'Noah and Lily have asked me to go on their show now,' she said.

'Good of you to keep me up to date with life in

the fast lane!'

'You think I've rung up to show off, don't you?'

'I couldn't blame you,' I began.

'No, Louis. I called because,' she took a deep breath. 'There's no easy way to ask this.'

'Ask what?'

She took another deep breath.

'How would you like to be my boyfriend?'

Chapter Eighteen

My New Girlfriend

'But only for twenty minutes, well thirty minutes, tops,' she rushed on.

'Poppy, what in the name of sanity ...'

'Just listen, will you? I've had some great chats with Noah and Lily.'

'Showing off again,' I muttered.

'About *you!*' Poppy practically shouted at me. 'I told them how you were savagely cut from my show on Christmas Eve.'

'That was really decent of you, Poppy,' I said quietly.

'I know. But I must have gone on about you so much they just assumed we were going out. And now they've invited us on to their show –

TOGETHER!'

'That's brilliant,' I began, and then stopped.

'As the show only has couples on it I don't think they'd have me on my own. In fact, I'm certain they wouldn't.'

I considered for a moment. 'It's dead frustrating, but I couldn't do that to Maddy ...'

'Oh Maddy knows all about it,' said Poppy.

'She does?'

'I asked her first. And she's very, very keen – says it's a great chance for you and me.'

'Maddy actually said that?'

'Yes.'

I relaxed quite a bit. 'So what exactly do we have to do?'

'Don't worry, you won't have to give me a big sloppy kiss or anything. We only hold hands occasionally, I suppose. You haven't got sweaty hands have you?'

'Never had any complaints before,' I said.

She went on. 'And we sit there with Noah and Lily and chat about us, I suppose.'

'Sounds cosy.'

'Louis, say yes, as I really wouldn't want anyone else to be my pretend boyfriend.'

'When is it?' I asked.

'Saturday afternoon ...' she began.

'But hold on, I'm not supposed to have

anything to do with modern inventions?'

'Don't worry about that,' she said. 'Ring Maddy and she'll sort it all out.'

'So what's Maddy going to do?'

'I haven't a clue, but my grandad will drive us ...'

'This is totally crazy,' I said.

'I know,' said Poppy.

'So of course I'll do it.'

'Awesome. Now ring Maddy.'

So I did. And afterwards Maddy gave me instructions as if I were in a spy film. 'Don't mention a word about this to your parents. I'll be round your house at seven o'clock precisely.'

'But I thought you were under house arrest,' I said.

'Lots of people from the American company are dropping by tonight, so I'll be able to slip away all right.' Then she added, 'Don't answer the door. Let your mum or dad do it. And leave everything to me.'

Chapter Nineteen

The End of Television

7.40 p.m.

At exactly seven o'clock the doorbell rang. I pretended to be absorbed in this card game I was playing by myself. So Dad answered the door. I heard him saying, 'Oh, hello, Maddy, Louis is in the living—'

'Actually,' Maddy interrupted and sounding like a very stern teacher, 'it was you and your wife I wished to see.'

Bit of a pause then before Dad managed to reply. 'Oh right ... well, we're all through here.'

Maddy, I noticed, was back in her school uniform – probably thought she appeared more official in it. Barely even glancing at me she said to Mum and Dad. 'Sorry to disturb you, but this is extremely important.'

Dad rubbed his hands together a bit uncertainly. 'Well, Maddy, make yourself at home.' Then he added very hastily, 'I mean ...'

'We are very sorry you are moving away, Maddy,' Mum interrupted, 'but I'm afraid it is impossible for you to live here.'

'Oh I know that,' said Maddy airily. 'I'm here about something much more important.' And she sounded so grave even Elliot's mouth was hanging open.

'Good evening, everyone,' said Maddy, sitting down.

'Good evening,' murmured Mum and Dad faintly.

'Thank you for your time,' she continued. 'I'm here – well you've probably heard that television will soon be a thing of the past.'

'We hadn't heard that, actually,' said Dad quietly.

'Oh it will be – any day now,' said Maddy firmly. 'The future is all with vlogs. In case you were wondering what they are ...'

'I think Louis showed me once,' said Mum unenthusiastically.

'I did,' I replied.

'Vlogs are where people – especially teenagers,'

explained Maddy, 'upload videos of themselves talking about their life and performing challenges. They might also do impressions or sing – so many things really. They now have millions of followers. And wherever they go they are recognised.'

'Not by me,' smiled Dad.

'Their fan base is huge,' insisted Maddy. 'And the vloggers take their responsibilities seriously. Some never switch off, not even at Christmas. Because on Christmas Day their fans still want to see what they're doing.'

'Very dedicated,' muttered Mum, but I suspect she was laughing inside.

'Well, the latest vlogging sensations are Noah and Lily,' continued Maddy, 'and I'm very excited to tell you,' her voice rose, 'that Louis has been invited to appear on a Noah and Lily vlog on Saturday afternoon with Poppy, who you may remember –'

'Of course we remember Poppy,' said Dad warmly.

'But why on earth do they want Louis?' demanded Elliot.

Maddy ignored this and looked at my parents, 'It's not your fault you don't know much about all this. It's easy to lose touch. But you must see what a chance this is for Louis. So will you let him appear on Noah and Lily's vlog? Don't answer me now. Think about it for a minute. Then say YES!'

I smiled at her admiringly. What an agent. What a girlfriend.

'Well thanks, Maddy, for that,' said Dad, 'but what have you got to say about this, Louis?'

'Nothing,' I replied. 'My agent has said it all.'

Dad looked at Mum. 'I don't think we need a minute to decide, do you?'

'No we don't,' she agreed.

That didn't sound very promising.

'On Christmas Eve,' said Dad, 'we were both very shocked when Louis was cut out from Poppy's show. He deserved to be seen. And that's why we couldn't be happier that Louis now has another opportunity by appearing on a vlog. Even if I still don't quite understand their apparent popularity.' He smiled, while Maddy and I grinned triumphantly at each other.

'There is only one condition,' continued Dad. 'That is, after the interview –'

'I go on living in the time of Stonehenge,' I said.

Dad nodded and then added terrifyingly, 'We are planning to extend our experiment by another week.'

This was truly dire news. Even Mum looked

a bit stunned as she said quietly, 'Oh, I never knew that.' But nothing could wipe out the really good news.

'And to further my education I'd like to come with you both on Saturday,' continued Dad. 'So how will we get there?'

'Poppy's grandad will take you,' said Maddy. 'But I shan't be going as I'm grounded until further notice.'

'But why?' asked Mum and Dad together.

'Just for putting a dead fish down the sofa,' replied Maddy. My parents looked at her, open-mouthed in shock.

'But I wouldn't be going anyway as Louis is appearing on the vlog as Poppy's boyfriend.'

'Only temporarily,' I explained hastily, 'then I'm back to being Maddy's boyfriend.'

'And don't worry,' said Maddy, as my parents were all but lost for words, 'this often happens in the show business world.'

8.30 p.m.

Rang up to congratulate Maddy on her brilliant work at my house (she'd managed to slip home without her parents realising too).

Then I said, 'Sorry I have to pretend to be Poppy's boyfriend on Saturday,' expecting her to reply. 'No, I understand,' but in a very sad sort of way.

Instead she laughed and laughed about it.

8.32 p.m.

She could have been a bit bothered.

That wouldn't have killed her, would it?

Friday January 24th

Poppy has just rung me to firm up the details for tomorrow and to ask if Maddy is still okay with everything.

'She's more than okay. She thinks it's hilarious,' I said.

Saturday January 25th

2.35 p.m.

Poppy whizzed her wheelchair into my house even faster than when she charges on to the stage. Following at a more leisurely pace was Poppy's grandad, who was dressed as if he was off to a cocktail party in the nineteenth century, wearing a musty-looking striped grey suit with a bright blue handkerchief peeking out of the top pocket.

Poppy's grandad had also been a magician several centuries ago. And he was the one who'd

166

taught Poppy everything she knows. She says she owes her whole career to him.

'And to think,' he said breathlessly, as if he'd just run all the way here, 'when I was a nipper and auditioning to appear on television, there was only one channel. And that was in glorious black and white. And it closed down for an hour every evening to give people a chance to put their kiddies to bed. While now …'

He gave a very wheezy chuckle. 'So many changes and all in my lifetime. What about that?' He smiled broadly as if waiting for us to applaud. Then he asked if he could possibly visit the bathroom.

'I think he's more nervous than me,' smiled Poppy. She thought for a second. 'No, impossible!'

Poppy's hair seemed longer and was all brushed down to one side, making her look a bit like a mermaid. She was wearing a glittering necklace and very long earrings.

'You …' I began.

'Yes?' she asked.

'Well I feel as if I'm meeting a star. In fact, you'll probably out-dazzle Noah and Lily.'

Then the doorbell rang.

To my great surprise, it was Maddy.

'I managed to escape for a few minutes to wish you both luck,' said Maddy.

'That's so good of you,' said Poppy, turning bright red.

And as everyone seemed more than a bit awkward I said, 'Well, it's great to be here with both my girlfriends. You're not to fight over me, now.' I sighed heavily. 'It's tough when you're as hot as me.'

Maddy was laughing away, Poppy went even redder.

'So have you two sorted out your story?' asked Maddy.

'What story?' I said.

'Your backstory – how you met,' said Maddy impatiently. 'And when you asked Poppy out.'

'We'd better work that out,' I agreed. 'Okay Poppy, we met at the final of *Kids with Attitude*.'

'Good to keep close to the truth,' agreed Maddy.

I went on, 'I was watching you make the king of hearts disappear so skilfully that I thought, here's the girl for me.'

'I like it,' said Maddy.

'Then so do I,' said Poppy.

'We'd better think up some really embarrassing stories too,' I said.

'Noah and Lily will love some of those,' said Maddy.

'I know, when you met my parents Poppy,

they told you all about how I got potty trained and illustrated it with photographs?'

Then Poppy's grandad shuffled back from the bathroom and announced it was time to go.

Maddy said, 'You can sort out the other details in the car,' before adding, 'I think you two make a great couple.' Then she sped away. We all piled into the car – Dad in the front with Poppy's grandad, Poppy and me in the back.

'We're off to meet Noah and Lily,' I smiled at Poppy, 'so let's just enjoy it, girlfriend!'

it's just a normal house...

Chapter Twenty

Mixing with Famous Stars

3.20 p.m.

When we reached Noah's home Dad exclaimed, 'But this is just an ordinary house!'

'What were you expecting?' I grinned. 'An alien spaceship?'

'Well, it's certainly a long way from Pinewood Studios,' said Dad.

Poppy's grandad laughed so much he nearly lost his false teeth. 'You haven't seen very much of Noah and Lily, have you?' he asked.

'I haven't seen them at all,' admitted Dad.

'Well, I've watched every single show,' said

Poppy's grandad. 'And they're all filmed in the lad's bedroom.'

It was Noah's mum who opened the door. She explained that Noah and Lily wouldn't be long but they'd been held up – yet again – by all their fans demanding pictures with them.

Dad smiled in a disbelieving way.

'They've done very well,' said Poppy's grandad to Noah's mum, 'your son and his young lady.'

'Do you know,' she replied, 'when Noah started making his little films I thought it was nice that he was doing something he loves – but I never expected anything to come of it. And it took a while for things to take off for him. But the moment he teamed up with Lily ...'

'They've got such chemistry, haven't they?' said Poppy's grandad.

Noah's mum looked pleased. Then she leaned forward and lowered her voice, 'I shouldn't really tell you yet, but soon they'll have their own clothing labels.'

'How cool is that!' cried Poppy.

'Oh, I'm the proudest mum in the world.' She turned to me, 'they gave you both a nice mention on their latest vlog, didn't they?'

'And I'm sure I'll watch it one fine day,' I said, giving Dad a very significant stare.

But he wasn't the least bit ashamed as he

explained, 'We're having time away from social media. We've already had nearly one week free from it, and we're feeling so much better.'

'Speak for yourself,' I muttered.

'And now we're planning a second week,' continued Dad.

'Wow! Wow! Wow. How creepily incredible is that?' yelled a highly shocked voice.

Noah had bounced in, followed by Lily who quickly said to Dad, 'Please don't be offended by my very rude boyfriend.'

'Hey, don't you go apologising for me,' said Noah. 'You're totally okay with what I said, aren't you, dude?'

'And you can't call people you don't know dude,' said Lily.

'What's wrong with dude?' demanded Noah. 'What do you want me to call him – mate, governor, or your lordship?'

I watched fascinated as Noah and Lily, without doubt the two most famous people I'd ever met, had one of their little spats that they were always having on their vlogs, right in front of me. I couldn't help feeling rather honoured to be witnessing it first-hand.

Noah was tall and super skinny with a loose quiff and a permanent wide grin. He was wearing his usual black shirt and black skinny jeans.

Lily was much smaller – tiny even – and very pretty, even though today her hair was yellow and she was sporting bright green lipstick. No wonder neither Dad nor Poppy's grandad could stop staring at her.

'I'm so sorry about this,' she said to them, 'but Noah thinks I'm getting boring.'

'Not getting! You are insanely boring!' shouted Noah, but he was laughing as he said it.

'So, he's asked our followers to give me these crazy challenges. And this is only the first one,' she grinned, 'to make me less boring. But Poppy, one thing Noah and I do agree on – just about the only thing, really – is that you scream 'superstar'.'

'You so do,' agreed Noah.

He and Lily waited for Poppy to say something. But instead she just laughed. Only a bit too loudly, if you know what I mean.

Were nerves kicking in? It had happened once before to Poppy just before at the final of *Kids with Attitude*. Was it starting again?

Then my heart missed a beat. Poppy was starting to shake and her eyes looked huge and glassy. No wonder her grandad was now watching her very anxiously. I reached out my hand to her, but to my surprise she quickly brushed it away.

It was just lucky Noah and Lily were busy questioning my dad.

'Got to ask you, dude,' said Noah, 'why would anyone ever want to live without social media? And I'm not being rude,' he said to Lily. 'I just really want to know.'

'Of course. I'll tell you,' said Dad. 'Because I want us to lose all the confusing clutter of mobiles and computers and concentrate on living in the moment instead.'

'However boring that moment is,' I muttered.

'And enjoy what's going on around us,' Dad continued.

'Even if nothing is,' I said.

'And anyway, does it really matter what's happening on the internet?' asked Dad.

Noah and Lily reeled back from him.

'But if you're not on a computer or a phone or online, what do you do all day?' gasped Lily. 'I really can't imagine it.'

'I wish I couldn't,' I said.

'I mean, I think it's adorable you are being true to yourself,' Lily went on, 'and following your heart. But I'm incredibly shocked too.'

'Well here's something else to shock you!' shouted Poppy suddenly. 'Louis and I aren't a couple.'

Chapter Twenty-One
Poppy's Shock Announcement

I wasn't shocked by what Poppy said.

I was TOTALLY KNOCKED SIDEWAYS.

Lily knelt down, clutched Poppy's hand, and declared. 'I knew something was wrong as soon as I came in. I'm very good at picking up atmospheres. You two have just split up, haven't you?'

'Well spotted, Lily,' I said at once. 'That's exactly what has happened. But Poppy and I can still talk about the good times though, can't we?'

'No, we can't,' replied Poppy.

'Oh. Can't we?' I said.

'No, because we never went out in the first place,' said Poppy.

'You know that's right, we didn't go out,' I laughed uneasily. 'My memory these days ...'

'I'm so sorry, Louis,' said Poppy, 'but I can't forget Maddy.'

'Who's Maddy?' asked Lily and Noah together.

'Louis's girlfriend,' replied Poppy.

'But Maddy was fine about it,' I protested. 'She really was.'

Poppy's grandad had his arm round her now while Lily was clutching her hand ever more tightly. 'Don't be nice to me,' said Poppy, 'because this is completely my fault. I talked Louis into it and—'

'I'm glad you told us the truth,' Lily interrupted, 'as we never deceive our fans. And as this is a vlog about being a couple, all our guests have been ...'

'We totally understand,' I said jumping up. There was really no sense in prolonging this. 'It's been so fantastic meeting you both. And now I'd get my coat if I'd brought one.'

Suddenly Noah half-pushed Lily towards the door. 'Listen folks, talk amongst yourselves for a minute, will you?' Then he and Lily disappeared. We could make out frantic whispering without actually hearing any words. Now what was happening?

I sat down again.

'You really think I've gone barmy, don't you?' Poppy half-whispered to me.

'Without a doubt,' I replied cheerfully. Then I squeezed her hand. This time she didn't push it away. 'Maddy was laughing about us doing this,' I said quietly.

'But didn't you think she was laughing a bit too much?'

'No, I didn't.'

Poppy shook her head gravely. 'You don't know very much about girls do you, Louis?'

Before I could reply to that shocking slur on my character, Noah and Lily returned.

'We have news,' announced Lily, smiling away at us with her dazzling white teeth. 'We might be about to do something we've never done before. This is because we so admire your talent, Poppy.'

Poppy lowered her head shyly.

'And what about you, Louis!' gushed Noah, 'forced to live a life that is totally alien to the rest of your generation.'

'So we could, just this one time, feature a celebrity with a good friend,' said Lily. 'You *are* good friends?'

'Oh yes,' said Poppy at once.

'The very best of friends,' chipped in Poppy's grandad eagerly.

'But we can only do this,' Lily paused significantly, 'if our followers agree to it.'

At once Dad started looking round. 'So your followers are nearby then?'

All four teenagers – and even Poppy's grandad – smiled at his innocence. 'Ah bless,' whispered Lily. Then she explained to Dad they were going to put the idea to their followers right now on the internet, and then see how many pushed the Like button over the next few minutes. 'Our followers,' Lily shook her head, 'You can never really predict what they'll think.'

We're all still waiting – very nervously – for their verdict.

4.10 p.m.
The results are in.

And guess what – we got tons and tons of Likes.

So it's actually going to happen. I don't have a clue what I'm going to say now. Especially as all that stuff we prepared earlier about how Poppy and I met is probably out.

But hey, who cares?! Poppy and I are going to be on a vlog with Noah and Lily!

4.55 p.m.

I carefully helped Poppy to get up the stairs. Noah and Lily had offered to record it in the kitchen, but Poppy insisted she could make it and added, 'It has to be filmed in Noah's bedroom. It wouldn't be right otherwise.'

As soon as we got upstairs I blurted out, 'Wow! Your bedroom really is even messier than mine. I love it.'

'If I tidied up even one single thing my followers would go crazy,' Noah grinned. 'That's my excuse, anyway.'

Poppy and I sat down on these little plastic chairs (which weren't massively comfortable, to be honest) next to Noah and Lily.

'Totally forget the camera. We do,' said Noah. And everything felt so natural – with just a webcam balanced on a pile of books – that I relaxed right away. Poppy did too.

The vlog started with a bit of banter about Lily's challenge. Then they introduced 'Our special guests – who are not a couple, but you so wanted to meet them anyway.'

Next Poppy performed a magic trick with Noah and Lily. Lily called her a 'total amazing knockout' and a 'complete inspiration'.

Then Noah said, 'You won't believe what's happened to Louis this week.' He briefly explained, before saying, 'Come on, Louis, tell us exactly what it's been like?'

'Well, my parents just announced one day that we were going back to live in the olden days. And then they took away my iPhone, my iPad and laptop and handed me an empty cardboard box and a jigsaw puzzle made in 1966 and asked, "Now isn't this much more enjoyable?"'

Yeah, I was exaggerating a bit for comic effect, but Noah and Lily were grinning so much I rushed on.

'So tonight when you're settling down to a computer game or chatting online with your mates, I'll be playing a four-hour game of Scrabble, or maybe going for a nice long walk in the howling wind and rain with my mum and dad. I may never recover from this, but you go on laughing,' I said in mock indignation as Noah and Lily were now almost falling off their chairs from laughing so much at me. And I could feel the adrenalin rushing through me just as I do when I'm telling jokes.

The vlog ended with Noah and Lily's laughter still ringing in my ears. Afterwards I thought Poppy might be a bit mad at me for taking up so much time. But she only said to me, 'Tonight you were even funnier than when you were on my show.'

5.10 p.m.
Back home and I've rung Maddy. Told her how the vlog went, and then asked. 'Poppy was wrong, wasn't she? You weren't bothered about today, were you?'

Maddy hesitated. 'If I had to pretend to be Edgar's girlfriend, how would you feel?'

'I'd completely hate it,' I said at once. 'But Maddy, you were laughing about it.'

'You forget, Louis, I have acted in school plays.'

And I had forgotten that.

'I didn't want you to guess how I really felt,' said Maddy, 'as it's a huge chance for you. But when I saw you going off with Poppy, who was looking especially lovely today, that knot in my stomach grew tighter and tighter.'

'And I totally missed it,' I said. 'I'm sorry.'

'Don't feel bad,' replied Maddy. 'Only a girl would spot that.'

7.40 p.m.
Maddy rang. Poppy has texted her that the vlog is up and that I'm 'brilliant'. She's watched it twice already. 'Louis the Laugh is back. I so wish you could see it.'

*   *   *

181

8.05 p.m.

Asked Dad if I could watch that one vlog if I promised to switch the computer right off straight after. 'I swear on Elliot's life, I will,' I said.

Dad paused. I think Mum was looking at him quite hopefully too. But then he smiled regretfully. 'But once we start doing that – well, I really don't want to break the spell.'

What spell!

'Of course, as soon as our experiment is over we can watch it over and over.'

'When exactly will this experiment be finished?' I groaned.

'We'll let you know,' said Dad.

Sunday January 26th

5.00 p.m.

Nan and Grandad are back from their winter cruise and have just paid us a visit. They always sit very straight on our sofa, like royalty granting us an audience.

Cosy, apple-cheeked, smiley grandparents they're not.

No, they're the kind who will ask you your times tables and look angry when you don't know the answer instantly. They're not big fans of modern life either. So I assumed they'd be madly keen about Dad's crazy idea. Instead they seemed more amused by it.

'Have you had an enjoyable week, Louis?' asked Nan.

'In a word, no. In fact right now there's no more boring place in the world than my house.'

'But Elliot told me he's having such a good time,' said Nan.

'Elliot's a lunatic,' I said, 'and changes his mind ninety times a minute.' Right now, Elliot was at a birthday party and being missed by no one.

Then Mum and Dad bounded in. 'Do you know,' asked Dad, 'what's been so fantastic about this week? We're all talking so much more.'

'No, you're talking so much more and we have to listen,' I said. Then I turned to Nan and Grandad. 'Can you tell me where Dad's off switch is?'

I thought they'd tell me off for being cheeky, but right then I didn't care. I was just so completely fed up.

Instead Nan said, 'Well, when your dad was living with us we could never find his *on* switch could we?'

She turned to Grandad, who gave a creaky laugh before adding,

'I counted myself lucky if I got two sentences out of him all day.'

Dad bristled. 'That might have been because you were always buried behind your newspaper.'

'No,' replied Grandad, 'it was because you never came out of your bedroom.'

'Nonsense,' began Dad

'It isn't,' shot back Nan. 'All you wanted to do was lie on your bed and listen to extremely loud music. We had to push you outside.'

'So,' I practically shouted, 'Dad wasn't leaping about the countryside every day, collecting conkers and climbing trees ...'

'Oh no,' interrupted Nan and Grandad together.

'In fact,' added Nan, 'I don't remember him ever doing that. And when he did venture downstairs he was always glued to his Walkman ...'

'Really?!' I cried, delightedly.

'We thought it was unhealthy,' said Grandad, 'having those big headphones on, shutting everything out.'

'Including us,' said Nan.

'Especially us,' agreed Grandad.

I jumped up. 'So Dad wants us to do things he never did when *he* was our age. He only imagines he did them.'

'No, things were really different then,' cried Mum.

'Oh, they were, Mum?' I said. 'Once you watched TV and listened to music all day, now we play on computers all day. That's the only difference.'

I smiled triumphantly at Dad.

He cleared his throat miserably. 'Hold on,' he began hoarsely.

Then the house phone rang.

It was an incredibly excited Poppy. Afterwards I told her news to everyone else. 'That was Poppy, she just wanted to let me know that our vlog has gone viral.'

There was silence for a moment before Nan asked, 'And is that good?'

7.15 p.m.

My grandparents have gone. Elliot is back. And we've all just played Scrabble. Only Dad's heart wasn't in it. I could tell. And afterwards he sank into a chair lost in thought. What Nan and Grandad had said hit him hard.

Surely it can't be long before we're back to normal now.

Monday January 27th

4.45 p.m.

You really won't believe what's happened now.

Chapter Twenty-Two
Mum Lets the Family Down

Monday January 27th

4.45 p.m. (cont'd)
Came home to hear someone chatting away in the kitchen. There was no mistaking that voice either. It was me.

How odd, I thought.

Am I throwing my voice without even realising it? I opened the kitchen door, only to spot Mum on her laptop, watching me on Noah and Lily's vlog. I'm extremely pleased to report she was laughing too. Well she was until I said, with a choking cry, 'Mum, I can't believe what you're doing, you naughty, naughty girl!'

Never have I seen my mum spring up more guiltily.

'You haven't just let yourself down,' I went on, enjoying myself hugely, 'you've let everyone in this family down. Still, you showed excellent taste in watching me.'

Then Elliot bounded into the kitchen.

'Avert your eyes,' I said, 'the shock might be too much for your titchy body.'

'Oh, Mum,' cried Elliot gleefully, skipping round her. 'You'd better go and sit on the naughty step now!'

'All right, you two,' Mum began, hastily closing the laptop lid. But it really wasn't her day. Just then the front door opened again, and this time Dad came in, accompanied by - of all people - Digby.

'Tell Dad what you've done,' taunted Elliot.

But Mum didn't need to say a word. Dad immediately spotted the alien laptop and stood motionless for a moment.

'I just wanted to watch Louis,' grumbled Mum, 'that's all.'

'And was he as funny as we expected?' asked Dad.

'Even funnier,' said Mum.

Beaming, Dad explained to Digby, 'Louis has just appeared on a vlog which has gone global.'

'Viral,' corrected Mum quietly.

'That must be a proud moment for you,' cooed Digby. But there was a faint edge of contempt in his voice. Mum heard it.

And she replied at once. 'No, the vlog has opened my eyes to the wonderful talent Louis has for making people laugh. Sometimes I think he tries a bit too hard with all his jokes, but on there he was effortless, downright ... hilarious.'

'Hey, thanks, Mum,' I mumbled, pleased and even a bit embarrassed by all this praise.

Digby gave her the most patronising smile you've ever seen. 'I'm sure when this wonderful experiment concludes, this young gentleman will have discovered many other even deeper, richer talents.' He raised a calming hand and his voice became very soft. 'I can still feel a lot of tension in the room.'

'All caused by you,' I thought.

'So I want you all to join me.' And before we knew it he was sitting cross-legged on the floor. 'Let's create our own bubble of tranquillity, shall we? And then we can ...'

'Actually, Digby,' interrupted Dad. 'Would you mind getting up? I think it'd be best if you left us to discuss this.'

'Oh, but I was going to give you all some advice ...' began Digby.

'Not right now, thank you,' said Dad firmly.

It was a great moment. Digby kept his 'I'm so wonderful' smirk on his face. But I'm sure he was quite shaken. And he told us there was no need to see him out. So we didn't and all gathered in the kitchen instead.

'I'll say it now,' declared Mum. 'There's something about that man ... he smiles too much for my taste.'

'And I bet he eats his own earwax,' I said.

Elliot began to laugh uncontrollably while Dad said quietly, 'I must admit I didn't like the way he seemed to belittle Louis's vlog appearance. And – I don't think life is quite as simple as he ...'

Dad stopped, a look of total horror spreading across his face, while complete joy raced across mine.

Standing in the kitchen doorway, was Digby. Seems he'd remembered when he reached the front door that he'd forgotten his umbrella. And he thought he'd left it – and oh yes, he had – in the kitchen. The awful frozen silence as Dad handed him the umbrella – well I wouldn't have missed it for the world.

When Digby did finally scuttle off – Dad made

sure he was right off the premises this time –
Elliot and I were sent upstairs.

'Mum's the one who's been bad,' wailed Elliot,
'but we've got to go to our rooms!'

'Don't worry, Little Legs,' I replied. 'I
confidently predict we shall be rejoining the
twenty-first century any second now.'

5.10 p.m.
Yet another family meeting. Dad smiled faintly
at Elliot and me. 'We know this last week has
been tricky at times for you both. But we hope
you've enjoyed it.'

'Oh, I have,' I said, 'apart from everything
that's happened.'

'We didn't so much want to live in the past
as go off grid for a while. I think it's done us all
so much good.' Then Dad's shoulders sagged a
little. 'Still, you can't fight progress. And change
is inevitable.'

'But no one likes it,' said Mum. 'Well, look at
you, Louis.'

I started, 'Me?'

'Yes, you don't like Maddy going to America,
do you?'

'Mum, that is totally different to what you
and Dad did.'

'Not really ...' she began. 'You must remember

190

that Maddy's father has been offered the chance of a lifetime.'

'According to him,' I muttered.

'But this involves him and his family making a very difficult change indeed. And it is also a wonderful opportunity.'

'For him, not Maddy,' I snapped.

'It could be for Maddy too,' said Mum softly and looking right at me.

'So, can I have my tablet back?' demanded Elliot suddenly.

'Yes, that's what we're here to talk about,' I said crossly.

Mum glanced at Dad for a moment. 'Yes, you both may.' She told us where the phones were hidden. Elliot immediately tore upstairs. I was about to follow him when the landline rang. It was Maddy.

And I never got a chance to tell her my momentous news. She was talking so fast I could hardly make out what she was saying at first. Then I couldn't believe her either. It was truly incredible. I quickly rang off and yelled upstairs, 'Whatever you do Elliot, don't touch your tablet!'

His head popped over the banister. 'Why?' And Mum and Dad sped out of the kitchen.

'Maddy's got a contact on the local paper. And

he wants to do an interview with us this evening.'

'Us?' Dad looked confused.

I explained. 'Maddy said everyone on the internet is completely intrigued by our trip to the Twilight Zone, and they want to see how we live now.'

'See how we live now?' repeated Dad shaking his head. 'We're not a freak show.'

'Yes we are, Dad, and it's brilliant, because now we're famous freaks and I'm totally happy with that.'

'And you actually want our experiment to continue?'

'Definitely. In fact, right now I can't think of anything better than to be lost in time. So how about if they see us settling down to a riveting game of Monopoly or doing a giant jigsaw when they drop by to interview us?'

Dad looked at Mum. 'Do you want to be a famous freak?'

She laughed, 'Why not? Anyway, I'm proud of what we tried to do.'

8.03 p.m.

The reporter, Bret – who looked about a week older than me – arrived just as we were all having an exciting game of Snap.

I suppose it was amusing, in a moth-eaten

192

sort of way, especially the way Elliot kept yelling out, 'Snap!' every single time.

When Bret wasn't laughing, he was observing us as if we were this new species of human he'd just discovered. 'I know our readers are going to be fascinated by this stunt,' he said.

'It wasn't – it isn't,' Dad quickly corrected himself, 'a stunt. It's our attempt to rediscover something very special that is being lost in modern life and give my family an experience they'll remember forever.'

I'll certainly never forget these past days. Much as I might want to.

8.35 p.m.
Poppy rang. Noah and Lily are 'blown away' by the response to our vlog.

'Everyone,' says Poppy, 'thinks you're hilarious. And they can't believe what your parents are putting you through.'

'It's not that bad,' I said.

'What!' exclaimed Poppy.

'Okay, it is. But you've got to remember that when my mum and dad grew up, computers had hardly even been invented. Well, not the ones you have in your home. In fact I don't think either of them have ever played a computer game in their life.'

'Neither had my grandad,' said Poppy, 'until I taught him. It wasn't easy. He was totally baffled by it all at first. But now he's always downloading games on his mobile and off the telly.'

I thought for a moment. 'It's up to me to update them, isn't it? In fact, it's every kid's duty really to make sure their parents don't fall behind. I mean, how could I have let my dad go through life without knowing how to destroy a zombie?'

'You really should have taught him that,' agreed Poppy.

'I know. I actually feel ashamed. And I bet Mum would love being a Master Assassin. In fact, she'd be a natural. You know what, Poppy, when they get back to normal the first thing I'm going to do is update them. And that's a promise.'

Tuesday January 28th

8.15 p.m.
Still eating breakfast when *The Times Online* called to do a phone interview with all of us. Now we're going national.

4.00 p.m.
Dad said the phone hasn't stopped ringing all day. And there are more people coming to

194

interview us tonight. By turning our backs on the internet we have become the most talked about thing on it.

So I've asked Mum and Dad if our experiment can go on into another day.

'We can't stop now,' I said. 'Not with the whole world watching us.'

Chapter Twenty-Three
Rules for Maddy

Wednesday January 29th

9.20 a.m.

'You're all over the net,' this girl yelled at me as I walked into school. She sounded both shocked and impressed.

Then some boys bunged their phones in my face (we're not supposed to bring phones to school but everyone does). 'Recognise these?' they demanded.

'No, what strange trickery be this?' I replied. 'I come from the dim and misty past, where we've never set eyes on anything like this.'

I'd kept quiet about my banished iPhone.

People at school think I'm weird enough already.

But now I'm a bit of an internet sensation, it's totally different.

2.30 p.m.

This supply teacher has asked me to stay behind. She said she and her daughter, Maisie, had watched my vlog (as I like to call it) three times. 'And every time you made my daughter smile,' she said.

Then she said her daughter would be so 'excited' that she'd met me and would I sign a 'sort of autograph' for Maisie. My best day at school for weeks.

4.15 p.m.

As I walked home, one of the neighbours called out, 'You're on the front page of our local paper.' I quickly bought one. There were all my family, laughing merrily, playing Snap. We are also this week's Talking Point. "Would you ever ask your children to live without new technology?"

8.25 p.m.

One of the journalists interviewing us tonight stated that my parents were 'an inspiration'.

And afterwards Mum said, 'So many people have said they admire what we've been trying to do.'

'I bet no teenager has,' I said. Mum had to admit they hadn't.

I do hope all this fame isn't going to my parents' heads. They're not used to being in the public eye. Unlike me.

8.40 p.m.
Yes, it's great being hot.

But not even my current hotness can make up for being permanently excluded from everything that's happening. Few of my fellow kids could stand that. Don't be very surprised if I end up getting some kind of medal.

But it's Maddy I miss most of all. The landline is total pants for real conversations. And in a week and a half she'll be flying to America. No, I still haven't stopped that.

But what I can put an end to is being exiled to ye olden days. And I don't care how many more people want to interview us. It finishes tomorrow.

Thursday January 30th

5.25 p.m.
Actually I didn't need to end it. Mum told us that she's been summoned back to work tomorrow,

so she and Dad thought this would be a good moment to finally conclude 'our fascinating experiment'.

'I think we've all learned a lot,' went on Mum. 'Your dad and I certainly have ...'

'Continuing your education, Mum,' I chipped in, 'I'd be really happy to teach you and Dad all about computer games. I feel bad I haven't updated you before. But there's still time. I'll be dead patient as well.' I smiled so invitingly. But neither Mum nor Dad seemed as enthused by my incredible offer as I'd expected. In fact, they totally ignored it.

Mum swept on. 'Yes, we have to accept change, but we can still make up our own rules when dealing with change.'

What was Mum wittering on about now?

She continued. 'So from today we will have no phones when we're eating meals. Instead, we'll have good old-fashioned conversations, just as we used to. How does that sound?'

'I'd rather be karate-chopped in the kidneys,' I said. 'And anyway what if we run out of things to say?'

'Then we'll have to eat in silence,' smiled Dad.

'Which means listening to Elliot slurping and crunching away – wonderful,' I said.

'But I'm looking forward to some sparky

conversations,' said Dad.

'Also,' announced Mum 'there will be no phones in the bedrooms for Elliot after seven o'clock.' He let out a loud gasp. 'Or for Louis after nine o'clock.'

'Mum, you can't include me in this. I've got hair growing under my armpits.'

'Oh yes we can,' said Mum quickly.

'So what are you going to do, come into my bedroom and say, "Come on Louis, hand over your phone like a good little boy, or you can't go out to play tomorrow. Here's a lollipop for you to suck instead?"'

'What a good idea,' Mum smiled at Dad.

I shook my head. 'You two are beyond amazing.'

'We'll take that as a compliment,' said Dad.

'One day you will thank us,' said Mum.

'Don't bank on it,' I muttered.

5.48 p.m.
My iPhone and me are back together at last!

I immediately called Maddy and told her how they want to take my phone from me every night. 'After hearing that news I'm amazed I wasn't wheeled out of the house in an oxygen mask. There are only so many shocks I can take!'

'They'll soon forget,' she said.

'I don't know if they will,' I replied. 'And you can't come between a teenager and their iPhone at night. That's a well-known fact. Well, sort of. Okay, I just made it up. But I tell you, Maddy, my carefree fun-loving life is just a memory now.'

'I've also got some news,' said Maddy. 'We're leaving a week earlier than my parents thought. They want Dad out there right away, apparently. So now we go this Monday.'

'Maddy, I ...' But for once words failed me.

'I don't want to go, Louis,' she said.

'And I don't want you to go.' Shivers rippled down my back as I said this.

'I have this horrible feeling,' she went on, 'that I'll never see you again.'

'No ... no, I just won't let that happen.'

'They have lifted my curfew.'

'Oh, big deal.'

'And I'm still not talking to them, which is totally annoying them. I'm even refusing to help with the packing,' she said.

'The packing!' I echoed disbelievingly.

'Yeah, people do that Louis when they move away,' she added. 'At least I'm leaving when you're the most famous boy on the net.'

'Probably a bit of an exaggeration,' I said with my usual modesty. 'But anyway, what does any

201

of that stuff matter without you here with me.'

9.05 p.m.
Now my phone has been swiped away again until tomorrow morning. Such is life in my house.

Actually, I think Dad was shocked I didn't make more of a fuss. But I was very busy thinking of something else.

Friday January 30th

3.00 p.m.
School is still buzzing about me. But all I can think about is Maddy leaving on Monday. There is hardly any time left for me to do something. Anything.

And who knows when I'll see Maddy again. When I'm grown up, of course, I'll see her all the time.

But that's aeons away. I can't wait that long.

Then, in the middle of double history I had an incredible brain wave. Even more incredibly, it was inspired by something Mum had been nattering on about.

But of course ...

3.05 p.m.
For my idea to work though, I had to present

a proper document – and make it sound totally official and boring.

Now who would be good at doing that?

4.50 p.m.

I think Dad was pretty surprised when he saw Edgar and me deep in conversation in my bedroom. We knew we had to move fast too, so we did. And when we'd finished Edgar said solemnly, 'This could change history. Well, Maddy's - and ours too of course.'

We are taking it round to Madddy's house tonight.

7.50 p.m.

Maddy looked shocked and happy to see Edgar and me roll up at her house tonight. 'You're all dressed up,' she said. I was in a suit and Edgar was too – he even had a waistcoat on under his suit jacket.

'My cohort and I have been working on something which will explain our strange attire,' I said. 'And we'd like to show it to you.'

We went into the living room. A huge smile beamed across Maddy's face as she started reading. Then her grin grew even wider. It was wonderful to see.

Finally, she said softly. 'This is incredible.'

Without another word she signed every copy and then sped off to find her parents.

I think they were quite surprised that Maddy was talking to them. So they half-ran to the sitting room. They looked a bit pleased to see Edgar – and not at all pleased to see me. In fact, I'm pretty certain their knees actually buckled a bit. 'What's that boy up to now?' I could almost hear them thinking.

'Please do sit down and make yourselves comfortable,' said Edgar to them.

'You both look extremely smart,' remarked Maddy's mum, smiling faintly. 'Now what's this all about?' she asked, sitting on the edge of the couch. Maddy's dad remained standing.

I began, 'My mum says, that change is inevitable.'

'Very true,' agreed Maddy's mum at once.

'But she also said we can make up our own rules for how we deal with change. And you can ring her up if you don't believe me.'

'No, no,' muttered Maddy's mum, her eyes growing bigger as she wondered where this was going, while Maddy's dad shifted about impatiently.

Edgar took over. 'So we have made up some rules on behalf of Maddy —'

'What!' spluttered Maddy's dad.

'On this document, which you'll see Maddy has already signed,' continued Edgar.

He handed Maddy's mum and dad copies of the document.

'In anticipation of your signatures I do have two pens with me,' said Edgar.

Neither of Maddy's parents replied. All they could do was just gape at what he'd handed them.

I'd like you to see it too.

But owing to the document's highly legal and highly important nature, it really deserves a chapter to itself.

Chapter Twenty-Four

This Is a Highly Legal Document
documenting that

Maddy will be able to return home to Britain during every single holiday (Christmas, Easter, summer) for a minimum period of seven days.

Her parents (herewith known as 'the parents') will happily and cheerfully agree to this and without ever being the least bit grumpy about it.

They will never nag about the cost either.

Maddy will be able to stay at the home of Louis for the duration of her visit. (Louis will ensure his room is thoroughly fumigated before vacating it, to sleep downstairs.)

If the parents do not agree to these terms Maddy has the right to continue to be unhelpful and uncooperative at all times.

The parents will never forget that Maddy is sacrificing her happiness for theirs.

This will be signed on the day of .... (date) by:

Maddy

....

Maddy's parents

....

....

and four witnesses

....

....

....

....

Chapter Twenty-Five
Amazing News

7.50 p.m. (cont'd)

The silence as Maddy's parents read the highly legal document grew and grew.

I hoped they were conscience stricken. But Maddy's dad didn't look very conscience stricken as his face turned a terrifying red. He didn't sound it either as he roared. 'All I can say is it —'

'This is very interesting,' interrupted Maddy's Mum. 'And I think before we say anything,' she turned to her husband, 'we should have a little talk about this.'

'Feel free to confer in any room you wish,' said Edgar.

After they left I said, 'Your dad looks pretty angry.'

'No, he normally looks like that,' said Maddy.

Then her parents returned. They stood in the doorway. 'We see you have signed this already,' said her mum.

'Yes I have, because I think it is a brilliant document,' replied Maddy firmly.

'My pens are waiting,' cut in Edgar.

'If,' and Maddy's mum really emphasised this word, 'we agree, will you talk to us about our new life in America?'

Maddy hesitated and I could totally see why. There was something about the way her mum said 'our new life in America,' which sounded like a twenty-year jail sentence.

But Maddy finally said, 'Yes, I will.' And Maddy's parents exchanged a look.

'Look, Maddy,' said her dad, 'of course we agree to you coming back to visit your friends. We'd always intended that anyway. From time to time we'll want to return too.'

'Excuse me,' said Edgar, 'but this document said every single holiday.'

'And for at least a week,' I chipped in.

'No, I'm sorry,' began Maddy's dad, 'we can't be tied down ...'

But then Maddy's mum added, 'Maddy could

always stay with one of her sisters. I know they'd love to see her – if Maddy wants to come back.' As she said this she looked right at her husband again.

And I knew exactly what that look meant. Soon Maddy would be having such a great time she'd forget all about Edgar and me.

Her parents don't know Maddy at all really.

Maddy's dad gave a heavy sigh. 'All right, we agree,' he said quickly. 'But we don't need to sign anything.'

'I'd like you to sign it,' said Maddy.

'No, I'm sorry, that's—' began her dad.

'Something we will do for you,' interrupted her mum firmly.

Edgar produced the poshest pens I'd even seen – I bet he writes his poems with those. And then he and I watched with a certain pride as Maddy's parents signed our document.

Next we added our witness signatures.

'We need two more witnesses,' said Edgar. 'Shall I alert your neighbours?'

'No, I think that'll be okay,' said Maddy.

And then her mum said, 'Thank you very much, boys, for your help, but we'd like to talk to Maddy alone now.' Edgar and I were practically bundled out of the house.

But outside we were triumphant!

'They can't go back on it now,' I said.

'Not now they've signed such a highly legal document,' said Edgar.

8.30 p.m.
Poppy was buzzing with excitement when she called me.

'Have you heard?'

'Heard what?'

'Oh, Louis! They,' and by *they* she meant the satellite channel whose name I vowed never to mention again after Christmas Eve, 'are making a last minute programme change and repeating my show this Sunday at 6.00 p.m.'

'Hey, that's amazing! I'm really thrilled for you,' I said, 'but will I be in it this time? That's the question.'

'Of course you will,' cried Poppy. 'You're the reason they're repeating it. You're famous this week. And if they cut anyone on Sunday it'll be me.'

'Quite right too,' I laughed.

'You don't sound very thrilled,' she said.

'I am. But I'm mainly electrified with shock.'

8.50 p.m.
Felt a lot more excited about it after I'd told Maddy. She and her parents are visiting a squad

of relations tomorrow. Then they are having a meal with both her sisters in the evening. But she will definitely be round my house on Sunday to watch me 'finally get the chance you so deserve'.

Saturday February 1st

I've just received an email from Evie telling me about the repeat of Poppy's show tomorrow, and saying how happy she is that I will be on it this time.

I showed it to Dad.

'You won't believe what else has happened,' he said. 'One of my contacts said he'd been meaning to invite me in for a chat for ages. Anyway he's been reading all the interviews with me and is very impressed by all the buzz I'm creating. But I've done nothing. Nothing.'

'Except act totally unreasonably,' I said with a cheerful grin.

'So we're having lunch next week. And he has a post for which he thinks I'll be ideal. I haven't a clue what it is.'

'Head of Time Travel,' I suggested.

'And all this because of something filmed in a teenage boy's bedroom.' Dad shook his head in total bewilderment.

Sunday February 2nd

9.20 a.m.
Maddy's very last day.

Chapter Twenty-Six
Goodbye, Maddy

9.22 a.m.
Yes, Maddy will be gone for a very long time.

Seven weeks and six days, to be completely precise.

But she will be back at Easter.

For one whole week.

I keep on reminding myself of that.

10.05 a.m.
Maddy has practically begged me to treat this like a normal day. She said she would much rather talk about me telling jokes on television tonight.

She has a truly noble nature.

12.30 p.m.

Maddy has told everyone she knows (and she knows a lot of people) about my TV appearance. She said that so many people have heard of me now, and they're dead keen to watch me on Poppy's show.

But strangely enough – or maybe not so strangely – I haven't told a single person apart from Maddy and my family. You know why, don't you?

Yeah, that's right. I have that horrible feeling something else is going to go wrong. So I'm taking absolutely no chances on another humiliation.

6.45 p.m.

So there we were – my family, Maddy and me – all sitting round the TV, exactly as we had on Christmas Eve. Only I didn't have my phone on my knee this time. Instead I concentrated on appearing casual and unconcerned.

Then at exactly six o'clock up popped not Poppy's show but Noah and Lily. Now what was happening?

In fact, they were introducing – first Poppy, who Lily said she was 'wild about'.

Then Noah rattled on about me always staying cheerful despite being forced to live in the dark ages. 'We know you're going to love

Louis the Laugh.'

Yeah, Noah had called me by my full name.

'And don't forget to watch Louis the Laugh on our latest vlog,' added Lily.

So now Noah and Lily were using me to plug their vlog.

ME!!!

Then they disappeared and there, once more was Poppy's show. Then, faster than I'd been expecting – there I was.

I don't know if you've ever watched yourself on television. I can tell you it's nowhere near as great as you think. You notice all your flaws for a start. Like my giant ears flapping about. I could have probably flown on to that stage. And in my head I'm so much better looking than that. And taller. And cooler. And don't get me started on my voice. I was certain it was deeper. Sometimes I sounded about a week older than Elliot.

I'd have thought I was a total let-down if everyone in my living room hadn't been laughing wildly. Dad kept saying, 'I'd forgotten just how funny you were that day.' And at the end everyone leapt up and clapped. Yeah, a standing ovation. Even if it was just from four people.

'You're certainly funnier on telly than you are in real life,' said Elliot.

And you know what, for the first time ever, I felt like a real, proper comedian. Yeah I know this is just a start. But hey, I have started. My dream, well, it's starting to breathe. This would be the greatest moment of my life – if Maddy didn't have to leave in just over an hour.

They have to depart for the airport at some mad time like four in the morning. So Maddy's parents are coming to pick her up at eight o'clock. (They had to be persuaded not to make it half past six, straight after Poppy's show finished.)

7.31 p.m.

Maddy is sure my comedy talent has totally returned – but to make certain she asked me to tell her a joke. And to make it harder she gave me a subject – ghosts.

So I was yelling out really silly jokes like:

How do ghosts like their eggs?
Terrifried.

And where do ghosts go on holiday?
The Isle of Fright.

And Maddy was calling out, 'Oh yes, you're back, all right.'

Then in the middle of all this my phone rang.

It was our local radio station. They'd seen me tonight – and were very impressed – and could they do an interview with me tomorrow evening.

'That is just the start!' cried Maddy, beaming at me.

8.15 p.m.
When Maddy's parents turned up, I said crossly, 'But it's only ...' Then I saw it was, in fact, one minute to eight.

Maddy's parents clomped about saying how different things were from their day, when you could wait weeks for a letter to arrive. 'Now you can be in contact all the time,' they declared enthusiastically.

This was true. Only right now that didn't cheer me up at all.

We all walked slowly to the car.

'Hope you've got the legal document close by?' I asked Maddy, while giving her parents a stern look.

'Oh yes,' said Maddy. I noticed she was also wearing the chain I'd given her for Christmas.

And then we heard someone running towards us – someone who was not used to running or indeed physical exercise of any sort.

Edgar.

He took a few seconds to get his breath, and

then he gasped, 'I have not known you very long Maddy, but that time has been golden.' Then he thrust something in Maddy's hand and gave her a hug. To my great surprise he also gave me a very awkward hug, before speeding off again.

'Let's never do that again,' I called after him.

Maddy was staring at what he'd handed her. It looked like a truly epic poem.

'Well,' I said, 'if you ever run out of loo paper ...'

'Will you talk to him occasionally?' asked Maddy.

'Stranger things have happened,' I replied.

Then Maddy's mum said, 'We really do need to make tracks now, love.'

I looked at Maddy. 'Just because you're scarpering off to America ... well, it doesn't change anything. You'll always be my agent.'

'Your *international* agent,' she said with a flickering smile.

'Exactly. And you know you'll always be my girlfriend too. However far away you go, nothing will break us up. You're still stuck with me.'

'Oh, Louis,' began Maddy, in a low, shaky voice. 'Me going like this it's so ... so *wrong*.'

And then we were hugging each other as tightly as we could. I was still holding Maddy's hand as she got into the car.

'Seven weeks and six days, that's all, until you return,' I called after her.

She gave my hand one last squeeze.

And then the car sped quickly away, and Maddy was gone.

I stood there blinking and shaking my head.

I was trying to shake off the misery that kept rushing up into my throat. But it just wouldn't leave me alone.

Finally, I slowly turned round.

My family were all clustered in the doorway, watching me anxiously. Dad asked, almost shyly, 'What would you like to do now, Louis?'

'What would I like to do?' I repeated. 'Well, I'll tell you … but it's crazy.'

'Tell us,' said Mum gently.

I moved closer to them. 'For the one and only time in my life I'd like to …' I gulped with terror at what I was about to say. 'I'd like to,' I said again, 'play a game … of Monopoly.'

'But of course,' cried Dad eagerly, almost dancing a jig as he raced to get it from the cupboard.

'And I want us to play by the fire, and have hot chocolate and those old fashioned cakes called fondant fancies, if you've still got any left.'

'We could always make some more,' said Mum.

'You realise this will totally never ever happen again,' I added. 'It's only for tonight.'

'We understand,' said Dad.

'And maybe after that,' went on Mum, 'you could teach us to play a computer game.'

I gasped at my parents, 'Really!'

Dad swallowed hard. 'Yes, it's time we learnt. Been on my mind to take you up on your kind offer for a while, actually.'

'Well, let's stop talking and get started then!' yelled Elliot.

As I took one last look round outside, it hit me all over again.

Maddy had gone.

But she will return in seven weeks and six days.

Seven weeks and five days in just a few hours.

MADDY WILL DEFINITELY BE BACK.

And maybe I will be too one day, as you've been top company.

Until then, always remember.

Smile on!

Your friend,

Louis the Laugh

A Note from Pete

I really hope you enjoyed reading about Louis' latest adventures.

How about sharing it with your friends? If you're not already a member of a book club, why not join, or even start, one? Book clubs can be great fun, and they give you a chance to talk about all the things you did (or didn't!) like about a book.

Here are a few suggestions of what to think about to get you going. (Of course, you don't have to be in a book club – you can just do it for fun!)

The book's title ...
- What did you think of the title of this book when you first saw it?
- Do you think your parents need updating? Why/why not?
- Louis says, 'I had to remember Mum was from another age.' Is that how you feel about your mum and dad?

Louis's parents don't like what modern technology has done to family life.
- Why do you think they feel this way?

- Do you think they have a point? If so, why?
- Look at meals for instance. Do you ever text at the table when someone has gone to the trouble of making you dinner?
- Is that being rude?
- Or do you agree with Louis – that's just how people live now?

How would you react if modern technology was banned in your house for a week?
- Think about some of the alternative things Louis's family do, such as playing board games and card games, playing with a Rubik's cube, going for long nature walks and having snowball or water fights. Which would you most enjoy?
- How do these compare with computer games?

Louis the Laugh is Pete Johnson's most popular character.
- Why do you think this is?
- Would you would like him as a friend?
- What did you think of the other characters – Maddy, Edgar and Poppy?
- Do you have a favourite? If so, why?
- Did your view about any of the characters – including Louis's parents – change by the end of the book?

Maddy's parents have to move to America – and she is forced to go as well.
- Did you feel sorry for her? Why/why not?
- What would you have done in Maddy's situation?
- What did you think would happen at the end of the story? Were you right?

'Eyes down on your phone is no way to experience the world.'
- How would you respond to that comment? Do you agree with it?
- Do you think the book has a message about modern technology?

Louis has a dream to be a comedian.
- Could you relate to that?
- Do you have a dream, or a secret ambition?
- Have you thought about ways that you might achieve it?
- What advice would you give to Louis?

Would you recommend *How to Update Your Parents*?
- What was your favourite part of the book, and why?
- Have you ever read any of Pete Johnson's other books? If so, did you like them?